Barren Revenge

Barren Revenge

JOHN PENN

A CRIME CLUB BOOK
DOUBLEDAY
NEW YORK   LONDON   TORONTO   SYDNEY   AUCKLAND

A CRIME CLUB BOOK

PUBLISHED BY DOUBLEDAY

a division of Bantam Doubleday Dell Publishing Group, Inc.
666 Fifth Avenue, New York, New York 10103

DOUBLEDAY and the portrayal of a man
with a gun are trademarks of Doubleday,
a division of Bantam Doubleday Dell
Publishing Group, Inc.

Library of Congress Cataloging-in-Publication Data

Penn, John.
    Barren revenge / John Penn. — 1st ed.
        p.   cm.
    "A Crime Club book."
    I. Title.
PR6066.E496B37   1990
823'.914—dc20   90-30187 ˙
                                                    CIP

ISBN 0-385-26534-4
Copyright © 1986 by John Penn
All Rights Reserved
Printed in the United States of America
September 1990
First Edition in the United States of America
BVG

Revenge is barren: its delight is murder,
and its satiety despair.

—SCHILLER

Barren Revenge

CHAPTER 1

"Look, sir! There's your wife," exclaimed Detective-Sergeant Abbot, pointing.

"Where?" said Detective-Superintendent Thorne sharply.

"Over there, I think, sir." But the bright yellow suit that Abbot knew to be a favourite of Miranda Thorne's had vanished in the crowds thronging St. Giles' Street in the centre of Oxford.

It was the first afternoon of St. Giles' Fair, a beautiful Monday in early September, with a blue sky and white scudding clouds, and a crisp Oxfordshire bite in the air. From the Martyrs' Memorial to the fork where the Woodstock and Banbury Roads parted company, people filled the wide street, laughing and jostling, singing and dancing, eating ice cream and candy-floss, crowding around stalls, riding on the carousels and dodg'em cars. Many were in fancy dress, mostly improvised, though there were a few professional-looking carnival costumes. Everyone seemed to be having fun.

The odd pocket would be picked, a watch stolen, a gold chain slipped from an unsuspecting neck, but on the whole there was little crime. Later, when it grew dark and the pubs were open, a fight or two might erupt, and it would be especially important to guard one's wallet, but for the moment there was a minimum of ill-will and the police presence was negligible.

Detective-Superintendent Thorne, a man of medium height, fair-haired, grey-eyed, with a neat military moustache, who was often mistaken for an army officer, was in fact a senior member of the Thames Valley Police Serious Crime Squad. His presence in St. Giles' that afternoon, with the cheerful, extrovert Sergeant Abbot, was in no way concerned with the Fair.

In fact, Thorne's mood at that moment was more suited to a funeral than a fair. The two police officers were investigating a particularly unpleasant rape case, and had been interviewing a suspect. Thorne was convinced of the man's guilt, but his family had insisted on providing him with an alibi, and until it could be shaken the police were at a dead end. Understandably, the Superintendent was feeling frustrated. And neither the crowds of pleasure-seekers in St. Giles', nor Abbot's remark about Miranda, had improved his temper.

Abbot said, "Sorry, sir, but I thought I saw Mrs. Thorne riding on that big merry-go-round." Some way along the busy, bustling street people were dismounting from the brightly painted horses and carriages of the carousel, and others were taking their places. "But I can't see her now."

"You never did." Thorne was positive.

It was true that Miranda had wanted to go to the Fair, and he had promised to take her this very afternoon—on what was nominally a rest day for him, providing "nothing turned up." But in a policeman's life social arrangements were always tentative, and linked to some such proviso. Things were apt to "turn up"—a circumstance which Miranda had surely learnt to accept as normal after seventeen years of marriage, Thorne thought.

Indeed, she rarely protested. While she was a friendly woman who enjoyed others' company, she was more self-sufficient than many. She always found plenty to do, household chores, gardening, reading, and since she had learnt to drive and had a car of her own, she had become involved with the Meals on Wheels programme for the elderly and sick. What was more, over the years she had developed a profitable hobby, devising acrostics and crossword puzzles, which she sold regularly to newspapers and magazines. This morning at breakfast, however, she had complained when, after a phone call from his Headquarters, he had broken it to her that he had to work that afternoon, and their trip to Oxford would have to be postponed, at least. Of course, Thorne thought, he had been working extremely hard lately, and they had had few opportunities to go out together, but still . . .

"Come on, Sergeant," he said abruptly. "We can't stay here all day watching this fun and games. We've got work to do."

"Yes, sir," Abbot agreed.

He waited for the Superintendent to take the lead. The two officers had come out of Pusey Street and were standing on the pavement outside Pusey House. In order to reach the alley by the Lamb and Flag pub which led to Museum Road on the east side of St. Giles', they had to cross directly through the centre of the activity, their way blocked by stalls and the milling crowd. Sergeant Abbot tried to hide his amusement as Thorne, having edged around a brazier on which a man dressed as a chef with a tall, white hat was cooking chestnuts, found himself confronted by a most attractive young girl selling balloons.

"Buy a balloon, sir. Take it home to your kiddy," she said persuasively.

Thorne, who had no children and had never regretted the fact, ignored the invitation, but Abbot gave the girl a broad grin. The idea of the Superintendent returning to Headquarters carrying a balloon was irresistible. Then, glancing in the direction of the carousel, which was beginning to turn slowly as it commenced yet another merry ride, he saw the yellow suit again. This time he had little doubt it was Miranda Thorne.

"Sir!" he called, hastening after the Superintendent, by now some yards ahead of him. "Sir!"

Thorne heard Abbot's voice and turned. He could see the Sergeant mouthing something, but nearby a pop group had suddenly started to thunder out the latest hit.

Deafened by the sound, Thorne shook his head to indicate his failure to understand. Abbot gestured. And Thorne's gaze followed Abbot's indicating finger.

At first he saw nothing to explain Abbot's apparent excitement, and he was about to turn away when he glimpsed the figure in bright yellow as she rode by, going up and down on her painted horse. The carousel was some distance away, and though Thorne's sight was excellent he was unable to recognize the face. But it looked like Miranda's suit, Miranda's dark curly hair, Miranda's shape.

Miranda? Thorne didn't believe it. It was someone who resembled her. Abbot joined him as he stood and watched till the figure came round again.

"It is Mrs. Thorne, isn't it?" Abbot said.

"No! Of course not," Thorne snapped.

Abbot opened his eyes in surprise. He failed to understand the Superintendent's reaction. Surely if Miranda Thorne wanted to enjoy herself at St. Giles' Fair, why not? Good luck to her! But in the next minute he thought that perhaps he could guess the reason for Thorne's annoyance.

The merry-go-round had once more come to a stop, and Mrs. Thorne—if it was Mrs. Thorne—was being lifted from her horse by the man who had been riding beside her. At least, it looked like a man, tall and strong, and easily able to lift her high in the air before setting her on her feet. But his head and shoulders were concealed by a carnival representation of some kind of bird, or so it seemed to Abbot at this distance. He wondered if the Superintendent knew who it was, and if that was why . . .

Thorne had turned without comment and was pushing his way through the crowds. Abbot hurried after him. Together they arrived on the far pavement and, passing the Lamb and Flag, ducked thankfully into the alley that brought them to the quiet of Museum Road. Here the sounds of the Fair were muted. There were few pedestrians and only an occasional cyclist. Thorne sighed with relief. The woman on the carousel couldn't possibly have been Miranda, he assured himself. He began to talk about the case in hand.

Someone else who didn't bless the crowds and noise of St. Giles' Fair that afternoon was Sir Leo Farling. Normally he did his best to avoid central Oxford, but an invitation to lunch with the Master of Balliol had brought him into the city from the peace of his country house outside Colombury in the Cotswolds. The Master was an old friend, and the lunch, lasting well into the afternoon, had been most enjoyable. Sir Leo was leaving the Master's Lodgings when he remembered that his wife had asked him to deliver a small parcel—a birthday present—to a don at Somerville. Somerville was at the far end of St. Giles', and neither of them had thought of the obstacle presented by the Fair. Nevertheless, Sir Leo wasn't prepared to be deterred by it.

Sir Leo was a tall man in his early sixties. After a distinguished career at the bar, he had been a judge for several years. His main hobby was the cultivation of orchids, and the display in his heated greenhouses was well known. More actively, he played golf with a single-figure handicap, and a good game of tennis. He swam daily in his heated pool. If possible, he preferred to walk rather than drive, and Somerville was only a short distance from Balliol.

He had reckoned it would take him about fifteen minutes to reach his goal, deliver the package and return to the Broad, where his car was parked. In fact, compelled to force a passage through and around the merry-makers, he took almost that amount of time to get to Somerville, and by then his temper was beginning to fray.

He set off on the return journey, determined to get away from the crush as soon as possible. If he had been

more aware of his surroundings he might have seen
Detective-Superintendent Thorne, whom he had met occasionally, disappearing by the Lamb and Flag with Sergeant Abbot. He might also have noticed Eddie Mull, for
he had fairly recently sent Eddie's brother to prison for a
stiff term. But at this point he was single-minded, caring
only about reaching his car and getting out of the city.

As he reached the Martyrs' Memorial, Sir Leo was able
to lengthen his stride. The crowd was thinner here, on the
edge of the Fair, and he was able to hurry along beside
Balliol until he reached the Broad. He was in sight of his
car when he smelt burning. He stopped, sniffed and went
on. The smell went with him, and it got stronger. He
stopped again and looked down at his person.

Smoke was coming from the pocket of his jacket. He
plunged in his hand and yelped with pain as he touched
something burning hot. A black-ringed hole was beginning to appear in the material, and he realized that unless
he acted quickly he would literally be on fire. He stripped
off his jacket, dropped it on the pavement and started to
stamp on the burning area. He heard something crack
and became even more annoyed when he saw the dark
ink stain seep through the cloth from his broken pen.

One or two passers-by grinned at him, and one or two
hesitated, but it was clear that he was in no danger, and no
one stopped. Finally Sir Leo picked up his jacket and was
regarding it ruefully, swallowing an oath, as a porter
emerged from Trinity College lodge and came up to him.

"I saw you from the window. You're all right, aren't you,
sir?"

"I'm all right, yes, but that's more than anyone can say
for my suit. The jacket's ruined."

The porter shook his head in sympathy. "Bad luck, sir."

"What's luck got to do with it?"

The man stared at him. "I—I thought, a pipe, a cigarette . . ." He left the sentence unfinished.

Sir Leo was carefully inspecting what remained of his

pocket. "No, not a pipe," he said, "nor a cigarette. Look. One of those little cigars, going well and guaranteed to set light to the material. And it so happens I don't smoke. Someone must have slipped it into my pocket deliberately when I was walking through the Fair."

"But that's bloody dangerous, sir! That's criminal! Someone ought to be arrested."

Sir Leo smiled sardonically. "First catch your man—"

His jacket over his arm, Sir Leo nodded farewell to the porter, and crossed to his car. He unlocked the door, got behind the wheel and put the jacket on the seat beside him. He sat there for a full minute before starting the engine. He felt oddly shaken.

There had been no real danger. He had been bound to notice the fire before his clothes were properly alight. Nor was the damage great—a slightly burnt hand and a jacket with a hole in it, which his tailor could readily replace. But it was an unpleasant incident. He wondered if he had been recognized and the trick had been deliberate, or if he were merely a chance victim. The odds seemed about even.

Finally, realizing that the Trinity porter was still watching him with some anxiety, Sir Leo started the car and drove off. His wife would see the jacket, and he would have to tell her about it, but he decided to make light of the matter. Nothing could be done to find the culprit and there was no point in worrying. The whole thing was best forgotten.

It was after five by the time Superintendent Thorne and Sergeant Abbot returned to the Headquarters of the Thames Valley Police at Kidlington, just outside Oxford. Abbot was going off duty, but George Thorne knew he had a couple of hours of paperwork ahead of him.

The officers' dining-room was shut, so he went first to the canteen, where he ordered a pot of tea and some buttered toast. Not feeling sociable, he took his tray to an empty table where he gazed morosely out of the window as he ate. No one interrupted him, so he was alone with his thoughts. He tried to concentrate on the rape case, but his mind kept wandering to Miranda. He couldn't decide whether or not to phone her.

Why not? he asked himself. He would normally, if only to warn her that he would be home late. His hesitation was stupid, he thought. There was no need to worry because he'd seen someone like her in Oxford that afternoon.

George Thorne finished his tea, carefully wiped his moustache on a paper napkin and went along the corridor to his office. Once there he waited no longer. He got an outside line, tapped out his home number and waited. He could hear the phone ringing, and he smiled contentedly to himself as he pictured Miranda hastening to answer it.

But there was no answer. The smile left Thorne's face. Slowly he put down the receiver and began to make excuses. It was a beautiful evening, and Miranda could be at the far end of the garden. Perhaps someone had come to the door and, standing on the step, she hadn't heard the phone. Perhaps . . . He would give her fifteen minutes and try again. He forced himself to concentrate on his work. He couldn't know, but Lady Farling was having similar difficulty with her efforts to contact her husband.

Thorne was interrupted by a colleague with a problem and time passed. When he was ready to leave, he decided that it was no longer worthwhile to phone home.

CHAPTER 2

Earlier that Monday afternoon Stephen Crispin, Lucy Farling's boyfriend, had driven up to the Manor a few miles beyond Colombury in his old Volkswagen "Beetle," especially polished for the occasion. It was his first visit to the Farlings. He had never met either of Lucy's parents and, though he hated to admit it, he was feeling decidedly nervous about his stay, which was to last until he returned to Oxford with Lucy on Wednesday.

It was not a vast house, but nevertheless imposing, and it stood in fairly extensive grounds, surrounded by a high wall of Cotswold stone. The front door nestled in a large curved archway at the top of six broad steps, and Crispin, having carefully parked his car where it would not obstruct the steps, climbed them, put his finger rather tentatively on a brass bellpush, and waited. Stephen Crispin was a thin, narrow-shouldered man, with fair receding hair and a slightly worried expression, and he looked older than his thirty years. In fact, though hardly a celebrity, he was, according to the critics, one of Britain's most promising young novelists.

When no one answered the door he rang again, this time more firmly. He continued to wait, wondering at the delay, till suddenly the door was flung open and a man in dark trousers and a grey alpaca jacket stood before him.

"Yes?" the man said, obviously agitated.

The agitation infected Crispin, and he replied with less aplomb than he might otherwise have done. "I'm Stephen Crispin," he said, involuntarily sounding somewhat apologetic. "Miss Farling's—er—friend. I've come to stay."

The man seemed to collect himself. "Yes, sir. Of course. I'm sorry. Miss Lucy did mention it, only—" He said no more, but stepped forward to pick up Crispin's bag. "Please come this way, sir."

Crispin spent the next half hour in a pleasant drawing-room, full of flowers and chintz-covered furniture. He inspected the pictures on the walls, studied a collection of colourful glass paperweights on a side table and admired a set of ivory chessmen, obviously unused and for display purposes only. Then he sat and stared out of the French windows at wide lawns and flowering shrubs.

His mood varied between annoyance and surprise, as he heard hurrying footsteps and anxious voices calling to each other, though no one arrived to welcome him or show him to his room. And, more mundanely, he was hungry. His lunch had consisted of half a pint of beer and two sandwiches, and he longed for tea, if not something stronger.

Finally he decided that enough was enough and that he must make his presence known. He opened the door. As he did so there was a loud ring—clearly from the front door—and he saw first Lucy, then the houseman, hasten to answer it. A man with a black bag whom Crispin took to be a doctor came in. There was a minimum of subdued conversation, and the three of them hurried towards the rear of the house.

On her way, a clearly preoccupied Lucy caught sight of Crispin, peering from the drawing-room. She waved and called, "It's Jason, Stephen. He's desperately ill. We're afraid he's dying."

Crispin, who had no idea of Jason's identity, made sympathetic noises, but Lucy had already disappeared. He returned to the drawing-room and heard noises that seemed to indicate the doctor was leaving. Some time later Lucy came into the room, with a woman who closely resembled her.

"I'm sorry you should arrive when we're all upset, Mr. Crispin," Lady Farling said. "You must forgive us."

"Of course," Crispin said. He smiled doubtfully at Lucy.

"Jason's dead," she said miserably. "God knows how we're going to tell Dad. He doted on Jason. If that damned vet had come sooner we might have saved him. As it was, we hadn't a hope."

"Vet? You mean Jason was a—a—" Crispin stammered.

"A Dobermann," said Lady Farling. "A Dobermann pinscher. A marvellous animal. I can't imagine what my husband will say. For that matter I don't know where he is. He should have been back ages ago. I'm quite worried about him, too."

"It's all right, Mother. Here he comes now." Lucy turned away from the window at the end of the room which overlooked part of the drive.

The two women exchanged glances, then hurried into the hall. Once more Stephen Crispin was left alone. He wasn't particularly fond of dogs, he reflected, and he hadn't known that Lucy was so attached to them.

To add to Sir Leo's annoyance about his burnt jacket, his car had developed a slow puncture on the drive from Oxford, and he had been forced to stop in Colombury to have the wheel changed. Now here he was at last, hoping for some peace, but confronted with a wife and daughter who were clearly under stress. Quickly he scrambled out of the car as they ran down the steps to meet him.

"Hello, my dears. Bad news? I can see it in your faces."

Sir Leo had married late in life and, like so many men who do this, had chosen a wife considerably younger than himself. Helen Farling was in her early forties, slim and long-legged, her red hair without a tinge of grey, her creamy skin unlined. Often she was taken for Lucy's sister, rather than her mother.

Now she thrust her arm through her husband's. "Yes, very bad news, darling, I'm afraid. But at least *you're* all right. I phoned Balliol, and they said you'd left hours ago—"

"I had a puncture," said Sir Leo shortly. "What's the trouble?"

"It's Jason, Dad. He's been poisoned. At least, that's what the vet said was most likely."

"Jason—poisoned! How?"

"We don't know. It must have been something he ate, but he'd not been out of the garden all day."

Sir Leo, who had automatically begun to walk into the

house, suddenly stopped. "Helen, you said, 'very bad news.' Is Jason *dead?*"

"Yes, Leo. We did everything we could, but—"

"But if he's not been out of the garden—"

"The vet suggested someone might have thrown a piece of poisoned meat over the wall," said Lady Farling. "It's not very pleasant, I know, but the vet wants to have a look at Jason's stomach contents, I think he said. Anyway, if we don't mind, he's coming back to pick up the—the—body when he's finished his rounds, and—"

But Sir Leo was paying little attention. "You mean someone's deliberately destroyed my Jason?" he interrupted. "Poisoned an innocent animal? I don't believe it. My God, if I catch him, I'll—I'll . . ." With an effort he suppressed his anger. "Have you called the police?"

"The police? No, not yet."

"I'll speak to Philip Midvale myself."

"Philip Midvale? But—"

Lady Farling bit off her words. Philip Midvale was a personal friend—in fact, she and her husband were dining with the Midvales tomorrow night—but he was also the Chief Constable of the Thames Valley Police. She thought he might have more important matters to deal with than a dead dog, however valued it had been by its owner.

"Where's Jason now?"

"In the conservatory, Leo."

"I'll go and look at him before the vet gets back. Then I'll phone Philip."

"Dad—" Lucy began.

But Helen shook her head as she followed her husband and Lucy, who had just noticed the burn in her father's jacket, desisted. When Sir Leo joined them in the drawing-room a short while later, he had changed, and the state of the clothing he had been wearing wasn't mentioned. Most of his rage had drained from him by now, but his mind was still on the dog.

"Did they tell you what happened to my Jason?" he asked as he was introduced to Stephen Crispin.

"Yes, sir, and I'm—I'm terribly sorry."

"Dastardly! That's what it was. Dastardly!"

Crispin, who thought the word had gone out of currency in the nineteenth century, could do little but nod his head in agreement. In spite of Lucy, he was beginning to wish he hadn't come to this strange house, where the only thing that anyone—and that included Lucy—could think about for more than a couple of minutes was this dog. The arrival of the houseman to ask if they would like tea raised his hopes, but only momentarily.

"No, Carter, thank you. Much too late for tea," Sir Leo said firmly without consulting either his family or his guest. Then he added, "What we really need is a stiff drink, if not two."

And Stephen Crispin relaxed. This, he thought, was the first sensible remark he had heard since his arrival at the Manor. Maybe his visit wasn't going to be too bad after all.

By the time the pubs opened on Monday evening, news of the poisoning of Sir Leo Farling's Dobermann had spread to Colombury, though it would not become a titbit for the national media until the next morning.

The public bar of the White Swan was still almost empty. Two men—Willie Burwash and Bert Parker—and a woman, Jean Haule, who was Parker's married sister, were sitting at the counter, and a couple in a far corner were holding hands and making their shandies last as long as possible.

"I don't see anything funny in poisoning a dog," the barmaid was saying firmly. "How would you like it if the animal had been yours, I'd like to know?"

She was a short, square figure with fierce black hair and a determined manner, and she was addressing herself to the trio at the bar.

"Oh, come on, Madge," said Burwash, "he were the Judge's dog. That makes all the difference."

"Saved the poor brute from having to live with that bugger."

Madge looked up sharply. "Language!" she said, pointing to a collecting tin on the bar as the two men guffawed together. Parker was tall and scrawny with ginger hair and freckles, while Burwash was short, dark and muscular. They had been mates since their schooldays, when they had begun to get into minor trouble together. Over the years the troubles had grown more serious. Now, in their thirties, the despair of a succession of probation officers, they both had the pallor that comes from long prison terms. In fact, it was only six weeks since they had been released, having completed a sentence that Sir Leo Farling had imposed on them for armed robbery.

"You didn't have a hand in the dog business, did you, Bert?"

It was Jean Haule who spoke. A few years older than her brother, tall and red-haired, her resemblance to him was so striking that they might have been twins.

"Of course not, Jean."

"What about you, Willie?"

"Not guilty, Your Honour." Willie Burwash grinned at her. "Cross my heart and hope to die."

Jean Haule snorted. She was fond of her brother and had stayed in touch when the rest of the family had disowned him. Willie she found physically attractive, and on occasion they shared a bed, but mostly she thought of him as a second brother. It had gone without saying that when the two men got out of prison Willie as well as Bert should come and stay with her and her two children in the council house on the edge of Colombury.

"I hope you mean it, both of you," she said. "The Judge may be an old b. but I don't want any more trouble. I've had enough."

"He's an old b. all right," Parker agreed. "I wouldn't

have shed a tear if it had been him poisoned, and not the bloody dog."

"Nor me, mate. Maybe he'll be next. Let's drink to that." Burwash raised his mug. "And I know someone else who'd drink to it with us—except that it'll be a long time before he's sitting in a pub again."

"Poor Tony Mull." Parker nodded sadly.

"Poor Tony Mull!" Jean Haule was scornful. "He knifed a policeman. He was lucky old Farling didn't send him down for life. He's a bad lad, that boy, like all his family. In my opinion he deserved what he got."

Parker and Burwash exchanged glances. They weren't prepared to argue, at least not when their mugs were empty. Unemployed and, with their records, likely to remain so, they had little money to spend and were dependent on Jean for that extra pint.

Willie Burwash grinned at her again, and pushed his empty mug an inch or two forward. "We'll be having another, won't we, love?"

Jean hesitated. It wasn't easy being a one-parent family —her husband had gone off years ago—but she had a nice little house and a steady job as manageress of a clothes shop in Colombury. Things weren't too bad, even with a couple of children and these two men. If only she could be sure they weren't involved in playing dirty games with old Farling.

"Sure," she said, and called to Madge, who was polishing glasses at the far end of the bar. "Another pint all round, dear, please."

"And we'll drink to the Judge's damned dead dog," Parker murmured to his mate.

In the meantime, Detective-Superintendent George Thorne arrived home.

By the standards of the Farlings his house, though detached and double-fronted, was very modest, but it suited him well and both he and Miranda were perfectly happy with it. He didn't mind that the garage was single, and now that Miranda had a car he had to leave his own outside; there was plenty of space in the short drive, and his Ford was four years old. If he had any complaint, it was about the garden; in his opinion, it was much too big, and forced him to spend an excessive amount of his meagre spare time in unusually energetic pursuits. If he failed to mow the grass, Miranda did so, and his conscience invariably pricked him.

Thorne let himself in by the front door, slammed it behind him, and called, "Hello! It's me! I'm home!"

There was no answer. He went through to the kitchen, but there was no sign of his wife. Nor could he see her in the garden. He returned to the hall and, standing on the bottom step, called upstairs, "Miranda! Are you there?"

Still no answer—and Thorne experienced a sudden qualm of apprehension. Where on earth was she? Had she felt tired, gone to have a rest and fallen fast asleep? Surely his call would have woken her. Or was she ill? He took the stairs two at a time.

Their bedroom was neat and tidy, with no mark on the bright flowered duvet to suggest that anyone had been lying on the bed. George Thorne sighed with relief. But the room was empty. Thorne glanced in the other bedrooms, one of which he used as a dressing-room, and the bathroom before he slowly went downstairs.

He called Miranda's name again, but didn't expect an answer. The house felt empty; he noticed suddenly that the smell of cooking, which should normally have greeted him at that time of the evening with the promise of supper, was missing, and in the kitchen he realized that no preparations had been made for a meal.

Thorne didn't understand it. It was so unlike Miranda. She was almost always at home when he returned, and she always left him a note, or told him, if she was likely to be late. Never, in their seventeen years of happy marriage— the happiest of marriages, he reflected—had she failed to do so. But there was no message, and she had said nothing that morning. He dismissed the thought that he had indeed seen her at St. Giles' Fair; this would mean that she had decided—in a fit of pique, perhaps—to go there alone and leave him guessing. The idea was absurd, totally alien to Miranda's character and their long and close-knit relationship.

The garage, thought Thorne—of course! But the little yellow Mini wasn't there. So Miranda had taken the car and gone somewhere, and because she had left no note she had presumably intended to return in good time to get supper. But she hadn't returned. George Thorne shivered suddenly.

If she had been delayed—with friends, say—or the car had broken down, or she'd had a minor accident, she would have telephoned him by now. Or perhaps, he thought hopefully, she had phoned Headquarters and the message hadn't reached him, or they had told her he was out and unreachable.

Back in the house, Thorne went at once to the telephone, but there were no messages for him at Kidlington, and his hopes faded. He told himself he was being stupid, worrying unnecessarily. Nothing could have happened to Miranda. At the very worst—if she had been seriously injured in a bad accident, say—he would have been informed; she always carried identification. She would be home soon, with some simple explanation. Meanwhile . . .

Thorne didn't really approve of drinking alone, but tonight, he felt, was an exception. He poured himself a neat whisky, and took it into the kitchen. He wasn't a domesticated man. Miranda was rarely ill, so he seldom had to cope with meals for himself, and he eyed the contents of the refrigerator doubtfully. Finally he settled on eggs and bacon as simple and substantial. He reached for a frying-pan. Two eggs and three rashers were almost cooked when the telephone rang.

Thorne ran, to seize the receiver so violently that he
almost knocked the instrument from the hall table.
"Hello! Hello!" he said. In the background at the other
end of the line he could hear voices, and music. Immediately he guessed at a pub or restaurant, but he later realized that the sounds could have come from a radio or
television set. "Hello!" he said again, when there was no
reply. "Who's that?" He hesitated. "Miranda?"

More clearly than the voices or the music, he could hear
breathing—uneven breathing, choked, as if someone was
trying to suppress sobs, or possibly laughter. "Miranda?"
Thorne repeated. "Is that you, Miranda?"

For a moment there was no answer. Then there was a
noise that Thorne could only describe to himself as half-
way between a guffaw and a cry of protest. He fought
down his rising fear. The line went dead. His mouth set in
a thin line, he replaced the receiver and stood staring at it,
willing it to ring again.

There was really nothing to suggest that the call was
connected with Miranda. Instinctively he felt it must be,
but he told himself that logic was against it. His phone
number was listed under the name M. P. Thorne and from
time to time they got a wrong number or an obscene call.
But such calls weren't personal, related to his police work.
They were merely examples of the chance phenomena
from which everyone suffered these days. There was no
reason to believe that this call was any different. Yet . . .

Thorne caught himself sniffing. His mind registered
that something was burning. Then he dashed back to the
kitchen. The eggs and bacon he had hoped to have for
supper were a blackened mess in the pan, and blue smoke
was rising from it to make a dark patch on the ceiling.

Seizing the pan, Thorne removed it from the burner
and turned off the gas. Another couple of minutes, he
thought, and he might have had a fire on his hands. At
least he'd avoided that. But his supper was inedible. He
emptied the contents of the pan into the waste bin, and

put the pan to soak in the sink. These trivial chores distracted him for a moment or two.

Then he forced himself to eat some bread and cheese, and made himself a cup of instant coffee that he forgot to drink. By now it was dark outside, and he was seriously worried.

George Thorne didn't consider himself an imaginative man, but his imagination, such as it was, had begun to run riot. If Miranda had been taken ill or had an ordinary accident, he repeated to himself, he would have known by now. So, he reasoned, something extraordinary must have happened to her. Surely abduction was ridiculous? Or had she given someone a lift—something he had always warned her about—or broken down in some lonely spot? For a moment he visualized her stripped and assaulted and left to die in a ditch. Against his will, his policeman's experience supplied details that he didn't want to think of in relation to his wife.

Hands balled in his trouser pockets, Thorne walked from room to room. More than once he thought he heard her car and rushed to the front door, only to be disappointed. Hours passed, sometimes alarmingly fast, sometimes surprisingly slowly.

He was reluctant to report his wife as missing after so relatively short a time, though he knew his rank would save him from the usual questions and argument. But by eleven o'clock he knew he had no alternative. He lifted his telephone and called his Headquarters. A call was to be put out for the car, and all patrols and mobile units notified. The Superintendent himself would commence the unpleasant task of checking the local hospitals.

CHAPTER 3

"Female, yes. Age, between thirty-five and forty. Well nourished, generally well cared for. Dark brown curly hair, cut short. Brown eyes. No dental prostheses. No distinguishing marks. Had recently had sexual intercourse, almost certainly against her will to judge from the bruising and the state of the vagina."

Thorne winced. The description fitted Miranda but . . . "Clothes?" he asked. "What was she wearing? And jewellery?"

"She was naked except for a slip. Marks and Spencer's best. White. Bust 38 to 40." The intern's voice at the other end of the line from Abingdon was impersonal and slightly impatient. There was plenty to do in a busy hospital, even in the middle of the night, without answering questions that this—what was he? some superintendent? —might just as well have put to the local police who had brought in the woman.

Thorne had introduced himself as a senior detective officer from Thames Valley Headquarters, who wanted information and wanted it quickly. A detective-superintendent had the right to ignore red tape in an emergency —especially in his own area—and this, he had managed to imply, was an emergency.

"What about jewellery?" he repeated. "You didn't mention it."

"Sorry. No jewellery, but she's got bands of paler skin around the left wrist and the third finger of the left hand," the doctor said. Then he went on, "I'm sure you can deduce what that means, Superintendent."

Thorne was inclined to tell the doctor angrily that this was no time for stupid attempts at sarcasm, but he contained his temper and replied quietly. "That she usually wore a watch and a ring, presumably a wedding ring." He couldn't resist adding, "You're very observant, Doctor."

"Not really. I'm looking right at her. She's here, in intensive care—"

"Intensive care? Is she—"

"She's in a bad way, Superintendent. Didn't you gather that? There's not a hope in hell of talking to her, but if you just want to make an identification . . ." He left the sentence unfinished and waited. After a second or two, he said, "Superintendent, are you there?"

With a tremendous effort George Thorne got control of himself and his emotions. He had begun to feel physically ill as the full impact of the conversation hit him. All the time he had been telephoning, making his pseudo-official inquiries, he had been able to pretend that he wasn't personally concerned, for he hadn't really believed that he would find Miranda in this way. Now it seemed that he might have done just that, and he wished to God he hadn't.

"Yes, I'm here." Thorne swallowed. "I'll be along."

His hand was shaking as he put down the phone. It happened to other women; why not to Miranda? He knew only too well the stunned disbelief with which the families of victims learned what had happened. Some found it almost impossible to accept the facts of a case. As for himself, his feelings were in turmoil but his overwhelming desire was to get to this woman who might be Miranda.

He drove south fast. It wasn't far. The Motorway skirted Oxford city, and took him straight into Abingdon. The night-time heavy traffic wasn't sufficient to delay his progress, and he arrived at the hospital sooner than he had hoped. He parked in a space marked "Doctors Only" and went to the reception desk. He was asked to wait.

The wait was trying, and twice he protested. The second time he was insistent. By now he had convinced himself that the victim was indeed Miranda, and he was sweating.

"Detective-Superintendent Thorne?"

Thorne swung round. He recognized the voice of the doctor to whom he had spoken on the phone. The man was young and round-faced, with circles of fatigue about his eyes, but he managed a rueful grin.

"I'm afraid we lost her, Superintendent."

"Lost her?" Thorne said blankly.

"The woman who was attacked and raped. The one you were interested in. She died on us."

"Died?" Stupidly Thorne shook his head. He refused to believe it. Then he became conscious of the doctor looking at him curiously and he straightened his shoulders. "I —I'd like to see her," he said.

"Of course. She's not a pretty sight, but I imagine you're even more used than I am to seeing horrors."

Thorne nodded. He didn't trust himself to speak. He followed the doctor along the corridor and into a room divided into cubicles. In the first cubicle a still figure lay on a high, narrow bed, the sheet drawn up over the face. The doctor pulled it back to reveal the bruised flesh and the mouth torn on one side.

Thorne took one look, and turned away. So like Miranda! Or what Miranda might have been! But not Miranda.

For the next few minutes Thorne spoke and acted automatically. Somehow he managed to escape from the hospital, thankful when the doctor was urgently needed elsewhere, and thankful to reach the privacy of his parked car.

The night was comparatively dark, with a few stars and a moon in the first quarter. No one saw Detective-Superintendent Thorne lean against his car and vomit. Then, shaken, but feeling a little better, he sat behind the wheel and thought about his wife.

The fact that he hadn't found Miranda didn't mean that

she was alive and well, but at least there was still hope. He considered his next steps.

Eventually he edged his car out of the parking space and set off for home. When he turned into his street he saw a patch of brightness shining on the pavement outside his house, and as he drew closer he realized that there were lights in the sitting-room and upstairs in the bedroom.

His heart thudded against his ribs as hope surged. The next moment he knew it was false. He was fooling himself. When he had dashed to his car he hadn't bothered about the interior lights. The house was just as he had left it, empty, unwelcoming. Miranda hadn't returned to him.

George Thorne went straight to the phone and called his Headquarters. Nothing. Then he wondered what he would do if his wife never came back, if he never saw her again. He knew he couldn't face that prospect. Surrounded by the debris of his abortive attempt to prepare himself a meal, he looked at the kitchen clock. It was four in the morning—Tuesday morning—and his thoughts were in turmoil. He was certain of only one thing: he needed a drink.

Breakfast at the Farlings, as Lady Farling had explained, was a movable feast. Stephen Crispin had understood what she meant, but hadn't found it particularly helpful. He had intended to ask Lucy, but unfortunately the opportunity he had hoped for hadn't materialized.

At eight o'clock, feeling hungry, he decided to get up. He showered and shaved, pulled on jeans and sweater and went downstairs. There was no one in the dining-room, but Carter appeared almost at once.

"Good morning, sir. I hope you slept well."

Crispin scowled. The houseman's face and voice had both been expressionless, but Crispin suspected irony. "Yes, thanks," he said shortly.

"And what will you have for breakfast, sir? Coffee? Tea?

There's fruit juice on the sideboard, and cereals—unless you would prefer porridge?"

"No, thanks. No porridge. Just tea and—" Crispin paused, unsure what else was on offer.

"Very good, sir. I'll bring in the hot dishes as soon as they're ready."

Crispin was glad when Carter withdrew. The man had made it quite clear that the Farlings' house guests weren't expected to come down to breakfast so early and, had he known this, he would most certainly not have done so. The last thing he wanted was a second confrontation with the houseman. The previous one had been embarrassing enough.

They had last met shortly after midnight. Crispin, in search of Lucy's room, had been creeping along the corridor, fearful of every squeaky board, and dreading that he might bump into some unsuspected piece of furniture. The curtains were all drawn, and it was dark. He should have remembered to bring a flashlight, he told himself, feeling his way and swearing silently. It was too much to hope that in her own home Lucy could have openly arranged for him to share her bed, but he hadn't expected to be assigned to a room at the opposite end of the house.

He had almost reached his destination when a light blazed in his face. He could see nothing of the figure behind the torch, and he choked back a cry of alarm. Then a voice spoke.

"I'm so sorry, sir. I didn't mean to startle you."

Crispin's immediate reaction had been gratitude that it wasn't the Judge. But Carter, he realized, would also require an explanation for these nocturnal wanderings. He thought fast. There was a bathroom opening off his bedroom, so he couldn't use the obvious excuse.

"I couldn't sleep," he said at last. "I decided to go down and look for a book."

"Then I'm afraid you must have missed the stairs, sir. Allow me to show you."

"No—no. I've changed my mind. I think I'll just go back to bed."

Reviewing the scene in his thoughts, Crispin felt a flush of embarrassment rise to his cheeks. Of course Carter had known where he was going and why, though it was none of his business. Nevertheless, given a choice, he would have preferred to avoid a tête-à-tête with the man first thing next morning.

Crispin drank a large glass of orange juice, and ate some muesli. The houseman returned with the tea, and was arranging dishes on a hotplate when Lucy came in.

Ignoring the houseman, she said at once, "What on earth happened to you last night, Stephen? I fell asleep waiting for you."

"I—I'm sorry, but—"

At this point Carter, with somewhat blatantly obvious tact, found it necessary to leave the dining-room, and Crispin was able to explain. Lucy laughed aloud. "Just like a French farce," she said. Then, when she had recovered from her amusement, she added, "I wonder what Carter was doing, sneaking around the house like that in the middle of the night." It was a question that hadn't yet occurred to Crispin.

Nor was there any chance to pursue it before Sir Leo arrived. He was wearing a towelling robe and canvas sneakers, having come straight from his morning swim. In spite of this he seemed to regard the younger man with a certain amount of disapproval.

"You're up early—er—Stephen?" he said. Lucy had insisted at their initial meeting the previous day that her parents should call Crispin by his first name.

"I wasn't quite sure of the form, sir," Crispin replied a little hesitantly, realizing that he sounded like a school-boy. He turned to Lucy for help, but, with a slight smile on her face, she was busy cutting the top off a boiled egg. She might be a little more cooperative, he thought. She knew the details of his lifestyle only too well—a two-room flat in

North Oxford, struggling with his third novel, reviewing
the occasional book, coaching in order to eke out the
money he earned from his writing. It was very different
from Lucy's own way of living—post-graduate research in
one of Oxford's most prestigious colleges, with a father to
support her and a country house for weekends.

"Well, what do you have in mind for this morning?" Sir
Leo asked finally.

Crispin tried to adjust his attitude. "I was hoping Lucy
would take me for a walk, sir," he replied.

Lucy nodded her agreement, though Sir Leo made no
reply. Taking the absence of continued conversation as a
dismissal, Stephen Crispin hurriedly finished his tea and
excused himself.

A while later he was strolling down the drive with Lucy.
They turned left on the road, and eventually on to a lane.
Lucy took his hand and pulled him towards her. She
kissed him hard. "That's for last night, poor boy," she said.
Crispin grinned in response. It was another perfect September day, cool but sunny, and Crispin, urban type that
he was, soon found he was enjoying himself.

Lucy pointed to some blackberries growing in the
hedgerow, and contentedly they ate a few. In search of
others, they turned off the lane on to what was little more
than a track that ran along the top of a hill. On their right
was an open field planted with some crop Crispin failed to
recognize, and on his left was the wall that bounded Sir
Leo Farling's property. Pleasantly conscious of their surroundings, they strolled on.

At one point, as they stopped to admire the view of
rolling downs, dotted with woods and the occasional
house of creamy stone, Crispin suddenly became aware of
an angry buzzing. He looked about him. It seemed to
come from above, but there was nothing to be seen there
but the hazy blue sky.

"What the hell's that noise?" he said.

It took them a little while to realize that the source of

the sound was an elm tree on the other side of the wall, and they had to step back into the field before they could make out what was happening. A swarm of flies and blue-bottles was seething around some object caught between the branches in a fork of the tree. Crispin couldn't explain why he bent, picked up a clod of earth and threw it at the insects. It disturbed them sufficiently to see that what they found so exciting was a large piece of meat.

It was only half an hour before a reluctant Stephen Crispin, urged on by Sir Leo and watched with some anxiety by Lucy and Lady Farling, was climbing up the elm tree. It was vitally important, Sir Leo had said, to collect evidence that might show who had poisoned Jason.

"Up a tree?" Lady Farling had exclaimed in surprise.

"Don't be silly," Sir Leo had replied. "Probably a first attempt. It lodged in the tree and he tried again with another bit."

"I see," Lady Farling had said, a little dubiously.

In any case, the bluebottles were now buzzing round Crispin's head, while the smell of the rotting meat nause-ated him. He broke off a small branch, poked at the meat, dislodged it and watched it fall. Sir Leo was waiting to pounce, with a large piece of newspaper in his hands.

"Splendid!" he said.

It was the only word of commendation or thanks that Crispin was to receive. By the time he had slithered down the tree, his hands grazed and his new jeans torn, the group had been joined by a police sergeant called Court who had arrived from Colombury, together with a consta-ble. Lady Farling had managed to persuade her husband that he shouldn't disturb the Chief Constable, but Sir Leo had been determined to call at least the local police as soon as he learnt that some evidence existed.

"Find the butcher," Sir Leo said, handing the smelly parcel to the Sergeant. "That should give you a lead. And look for footprints and any other signs on the other side of the wall."

As Sergeant Court eyed the package somewhat doubt-fully and hastily handed it to the constable, Sir Leo contin-ued with his instructions. For his part, Crispin went back to the house in a somewhat disgruntled mood. His jeans were ruined and, like his hands, his shoes were badly scratched. It was turning out to be an expensive visit, he thought sadly.

CHAPTER 4

At about the time that Stephen Crispin was climbing his elm tree, George Thorne was awakened by his telephone. He lifted his head from a cushion, opened his eyes and made to sit up, only to sink back again as his stomach heaved, a blinding pain cut through his head and the room began to slide sideways. He shut his eyes tight.

Too much whisky, he thought at once, and no food. He tried opening his eyes again, slowly and carefully, and could see bright daylight outside. He managed to focus on his watch as he reached for the phone. It was nearly eleven; he must have slept for five or six hours. He real-ized he was lying on the sofa in his sitting-room. The curtains were not drawn, the lamps were still lit and he was fully dressed in the clothes he had worn yesterday.

By now memories—most unpleasant memories—had come flooding back. Drunk, he thought with disgust. Drunk. Yet, if ever a man had an excuse, surely it was he. Where in God's name was Miranda? What on earth had happened to her? For a moment he wondered if by any chance she had returned overnight, though surely she would have done her best to rouse him, and explain.

George Thorne groaned aloud. He would have liked to stay where he was for ever, but he knew this was irra-tional. With great care he sat up and shifted his legs on to the floor. The room swayed, but he found he was able to stand up slowly. Staggering a little, he made his way upstairs. No. As he had expected, the house was empty, except for himself.

As he came down again, very carefully, the phone which had ceased to ring started again. It was Abbot at the other end of the line, asking when he would be coming into Headquarters. "Give me an hour or so," said Thorne. "I've got things to attend to here."

His wits were beginning to return. First things first, he thought. Black coffee and dry toast. In the kitchen he put on the kettle and bent to get the bread out of the refrigerator. But, as he straightened, his stomach suddenly knotted and, dropping the loaf, he ran for the cloakroom.

Ashamed, he knelt on the floor in front of the lavatory pan and retched. Lack of food meant that he brought up only an evil-smelling liquid that left an awful aftertaste of sour whisky on his tongue. The paroxysm had shaken him, but after a while he felt better and was able to get up and rinse his mouth with cold water. That helped, too, though the sight of his grey, unshaven face in the mirror over the washbasin did nothing for his morale.

Grimly he returned to the kitchen, made coffee and toast and forced himself to eat and drink. Then he went upstairs, to strip off his clothes and run himself a hot bath. Shaving was difficult; his hand was shaking slightly and he cut himself twice.

But the very normality of the routine—bathing, shaving, dressing—soothed him, and his professional instincts reasserted themselves. He'd been a fool, he told himself. Half out of his mind with worry, he had made no effort to be objective. True, last night he had taken some obvious steps, but there were others which simply hadn't occurred to him then.

He found himself hesitating outside the door of the bedroom he shared with Miranda. The idea that she had simply walked out on him was absurd, but it was one that would certainly occur to his colleagues, especially if Abbot had reported his notion that she had been at St. Giles' Fair, and apparently with another man. He cringed as he thought of the sniggers that would pass around Headquarters; he was fully aware that his devotion to Miranda was well known.

Inside the room he stood in front of his wife's built-in wardrobe, conscious of the scent of the toilet water she used. He pushed back the sliding doors. Miranda Thorne liked clothes, but her taste was eclectic. She always chose well-cut garments in bright clear colours. Such outfits were sometimes expensive, but she wore them for ages, and never seemed to grow tired of them. Nor did she buy a great many; extravagance had never been one of her vices. On the contrary.

The Superintendent stared in dismay at the almost empty wardrobe, then turned quickly to the chest of drawers built in beside it. This too was equally empty; as far as Thorne could judge, all the newer things had gone, though it was difficult to be certain. Then he noticed that Miranda's jewel box, which usually stood on top of her dressing-table, was missing, as were the brush and comb she always used, and most of her cosmetics. On the floor beneath the dressing-table he saw the gold neck chain he had given her, which she had liked so much. He picked it up and put it on a china trinket tray. Absent-mindedly he reflected that she must have packed in a hurry, intent on getting away.

Then, "Packed!" he thought. His hangover forgotten, Thorne rushed downstairs to the utility room where they stored their suitcases. There was no doubt about it. Two large cases were gone, as was the square cosmetic case that Miranda always carried with her on to an aircraft.

Thorne said aloud, "No! No! It's not like that. I don't believe it. I won't believe it!" Miranda would never have left him, not of her own accord, and not without a word of explanation. If she had packed her possessions and gone she had done it under some kind of duress. But, looked at from an outsider's point of view—his colleagues' point of view—the evidence pointed in only one direction.

He hesitated for a moment, then went into the sitting-room. Though it stretched from front to back of the house, it was not a large room, but bright and comfortable. Miranda's desk was set in a corner by the window overlooking the garden, and it was here that she devised the crosswords and acrostics that she sold to magazines and newspapers so regularly. As usual, the desk was neat and tidy, with a vase of flowers, now needing water, at its side.

Forcing himself, Thorne went through the drawers. There were lists of unusual words, literary references, clues with answers. They told him nothing, and he wouldn't have known anything was missing, if Miranda had not remarked on Friday that she was part way through mapping out a particularly cryptic crossword. He could find no sign of any such half-finished work.

He told himself that the absence of a bit of paper need have no relevance to Miranda's disappearance. She might have taken it to the Oxford public library, for instance. Although the shelves on each side of the fireplace were largely filled with reference books for her use, she often required more abstruse volumes—especially for "particularly cryptic" puzzles.

Nevertheless, the absence of the crossword worried him, as he tried to plan his next move. By now Miranda had been missing for well over twelve hours. So far inquiries—personal and official—had produced nothing. He must report to the Chief Constable as soon as possible, but in the meantime he would get on the phone—to friends and relatives, even to acquaintances. He would have to be very careful how he phrased his questions; the last thing he wanted was to start ridiculous rumours. But he couldn't help recalling the yellow-suited figure in St. Giles' yesterday afternoon—and the man lifting it from the carousel.

"No!" he said again. "No! The idea's ludicrous! That wasn't Miranda." As he reached for the telephone and began to punch at the keypad, George Thorne realized he had been biting his lower lip so hard that there was blood in his mouth.

He noticed the day's mail on the doormat, and stopped to retrieve it. A bill, an obvious advertisement and two letters, both typed, one for Miranda, one for himself. His was from an uncle, enclosing a cheque, and wishing him a happy birthday next week; Thorne almost tore it through in disgust. Miranda's letter also contained a cheque, a payment for an acrostic. The "With compliments" slip was signed "With best wishes. Ian Dawson."

Thorne looked at it speculatively, frowning, before he turned to the phone, and a series of fruitless calls. Eventually he abandoned the instrument and left for Kidlington. He found his desk piled high with files, but he ignored them. Instead, since the Chief Constable was not in, he called for Detective-Sergeant Abbot.

Bill Abbot was unsure whether or not he should be pleased. On the one hand he was flattered that Thorne had chosen him to assist in what was such a personal matter. Clearly the Superintendent trusted him and trusted his discretion. On the other hand, he had worked often enough with Thorne in the past to know that his superior could be difficult and unpredictable, and the very delicacy of this case was likely to give ample opportunity for misunderstanding.

"We'll start with the neighbours," Thorne said, interrupting Abbot's somewhat gloomy ruminations. "Luckily it's only yesterday, so let's hope they remember something. The weather was fine; they might have been having a go at their front gardens," he added more cheerfully.

"Yes, sir," Abbot said, responding to the Superintendent's professional approach with relief. "And we don't mention Mrs. Thorne?"

"We don't, Sergeant. We're making inquiries because some—some jewellery and—and a few other things have disappeared from my house. Get people talking—that's the idea, as always."

They had no trouble in getting people to talk. As might be expected, the street in which the Thornes lived was not one in which the police were distrusted and shunned. On the contrary, whatever their political leanings, the Superintendent's neighbours—many of them casual acquaintances, at least—were responsible middle-class citizens and keen supporters of law and order. Generally, except when speeding in their cars or trying to find somewhere to park, they viewed the police as friends. No one seemed to think it odd that such a senior detective officer and his sergeant should be investigating a minor break-in; presumably they assumed it was because it had taken place at the Superintendent's own house.

Some doorbells remained unanswered, of course, but Detective-Superintendent Thorne and Detective-Sergeant Abbot received all the cooperation they could wish for from those they were able to contact. It was unfortunate that at first their interviews seemed to be proving fruitless.

At last, however, their efforts were rewarded, though in a surprising fashion. A Mrs. Canning, who lived across the road from the Thornes and some twenty-five yards further down the street, was recovering from an operation, and had spent much of the previous day sitting at her bedroom window gazing at the street scene. Bored with reading and knitting and watching television, she was eager to talk to the two detectives.

"What a shame," she said, when she heard Thorne's explanation. "Have you lost much?"

"A certain amount. Money and some of my wife's jewellery," Thorne said.

"A pity she didn't take it with her—the jewellery, I mean," Mrs. Canning replied. "I always do."

"Whenever you go out, Mrs. Canning? If you just pop out to the shops?" Thorne sounded disbelieving.

"No, of course not, Superintendent. Or do you know that was when the things were taken—while Mrs. Thorne was shopping?" Mrs. Canning frowned. "I thought you meant after she'd gone off on holiday."

"On holiday?" Thorne said blankly.

"Oh dear! Silly of me. I assumed it was a holiday when I saw her with her cases. She was called away, was she? Someone ill, I expect?"

Sergeant Abbot saw his Superintendent freeze, and the garrulous Mrs. Canning inspect him curiously. Thorne didn't answer her question immediately, and the silence was threatening to become embarrassing when the Sergeant hurriedly intervened.

"That's right, Mrs. Canning. Illness in the family. That's why Mrs. Thorne hasn't been told about the burglary yet. We don't want to worry her at such a time. We're doing our best and hoping we can rely on you instead."

Abbot smiled at Mrs. Canning beguilingly as he uttered this last, almost meaningless sentence. Though Vera Canning was in her forties and far from being the Sergeant's type, he managed to give an impression of respectful admiration. He took just the right line. "If you could tell us exactly who you saw at the Thornes' house yesterday and the approximate times, it would be an enormous help to us."

"I'll try." Mrs. Canning returned Abbot's smile. "I'm always ready to help the police, though, mind you, sometimes one wonders. When I think of that poor Taylor boy hanging himself in his cell, I ask myself what the police can have been doing to allow it. After all, the boy was going to appeal, and a lot of people believed he was innocent. He—"

"Mrs. Canning!" Thorne interrupted.

Nineteen-year-old Jack Taylor had been accused of smothering his girlfriend in a jealous rage after she had told him she was about to marry someone else. It had been one of Superintendent Thorne's cases, and Taylor had been convicted mainly on Thorne's evidence. In the Superintendent's opinion there had been absolutely no doubt that young Taylor was guilty of manslaughter, if not murder.

Mrs. Canning winced. She had jumped involuntarily at the sharpness of the Superintendent's voice, and had felt a twinge at the site of her surgery. "I'm sorry," she said. "I must keep to the point, mustn't I? You're busy men, and you can't stay listening to my gossip."

"About yesterday, Mrs. Canning," Abbot prompted.

Mrs. Canning hadn't seen Miranda Thorne leave the house, but she had seen her return about eleven-thirty. She had watched Mrs. Thorne park her car in the driveway in front of the garage, and carry in what she assumed was a bag of groceries. She had the impression that Mrs. Thorne was in a hurry, and this impression was confirmed half an hour later when Mrs. Thorne had come out of the house with two apparently heavy suitcases, flung them into her car, and driven away at high speed—much faster than usual.

"Was she alone?" Thorne asked.

"Alone?" Mrs. Canning frowned.

"Did you see anyone else—er—nearby? Someone could have been waiting for her to leave before trying to break in." Abbot did his best to make the Superintendent's abrupt question sound more relevant to the supposed subject of their inquiries.

"Well, Mrs. Thorne was definitely by herself in her car, and I didn't notice anyone else about at that time. The milkman and the postman had both done their rounds much earlier, of course. But I could have missed someone." Mrs. Canning smiled reminiscently. "I was watching Mrs. Thorne and thinking how nice she looked in that pretty yellow suit she wears."

Abbot glanced at the Superintendent, and then as

quickly glanced away. For a moment he had seen George Thorne's face, naked and vulnerable, and he was surprised at the rush of pity he felt for his superior. Poor devil, he thought, this has really thrown him; after this, he can't possibly believe she hasn't walked out on him, left him of her own free will.

But Thorne had gained control of himself, was thanking Mrs. Canning and saying goodbye. Together the two men left the house. Abbot expected Thorne to make for their car and himself turned towards it. The next moment he swung back, as Thorne was crossing the road.

"We'll try this side now," Thorne said, as if Mrs. Canning's story had made no dent in his faith in his wife. "There's a chap at Number Six, an army captain who was invalided out. He's often at home. And Crawshaw's retired, so he might well have been around yesterday, too."

At Number Six they found the Captain alone. Recognizing Thorne as a neighbour, he invited them into the kitchen for a cup of coffee and a slice of homemade cake. He, too, was ready to talk, but he could add little to Mrs. Canning's tale. He had spent most of the previous day in his back garden and his wife, who was a nurse, had been on duty. He had, however, seen Mrs. Thorne drive away.

"About noon, it was," he said. "I'd gone to the sitting-room window. There was a damned car parked right outside my house, partly blocking the driveway. It's often in the road, that car, but not usually in front of me. Anyway, there was a chap sitting behind the wheel, and I was going out to have a word with him. I thought I might suggest—tactfully, of course—that he move up a few yards, so that my wife could get in. Then I saw your wife drive by at a rate of knots and, in fact, the chap moved off too." He laughed. "So it seems unlikely he was your thief."

"What sort of car?" Thorne asked. "I've not noticed it."

"Oh, a Metro. Blue. Hundreds of them around. Thousands, I guess."

"You don't mean Mr. Parkinson. He runs a light blue Metro."

"No. This was a tall chap, dark, mid-forties, I'd say. Not a bit like old Parky. I don't think he lives along here."

"If you see him again," Thorne said, "say I'd like a word with him, will you? And try to get the number of his car. He might be able to tell us something."

"Will do. Sorry I can't be of any more help."

At the Crawshaws' Thorne told the same tale—a theft from his house, and his wife visiting sick relations. By now, Abbot thought, it was beginning to sound convincing, but it was producing no result, except to underline the now almost undoubted fact that Miranda Thorne had left of her own accord.

And the interview with the Crawshaws was positively embarrassing. They had seen no strangers around yesterday. In the morning Mr. Crawshaw had been gardening at the back, and Mrs. Crawshaw busy in the kitchen. Their two grandchildren had come for lunch, and in the afternoon they had taken them to Oxford, to St. Giles' Fair.

"Perhaps the theft took place then," Mr. Crawshaw said helpfully, "while Mrs. Thorne was at the Fair."

"You met her there?" Superintendent Thorne kept his voice level.

"Not met her exactly, Superintendent. We didn't have a chance to speak to her. But we saw her on the merry-go-round." Mr. Crawshaw was precise, a good witness. "She seemed to be enjoying herself."

"Yes. Such a shame," Mrs. Crawshaw agreed, "to get home after having such a good time and find bad news waiting for you. I hope whoever's ill will be better soon, and Mrs. Thorne will be able to come home, Superintendent. If there's anything we can do in the meantime—"

"Thank you," Thorne said shortly. "I'll be all right."

"And I hope you catch the thief," Crawshaw added. "He might have a go at another house around here. Too

many crimes remain unsolved these days. I suppose it's
not the fault of the police, but—"

The two detectives listened impassively. They had
heard such complaints so often they knew them by heart.
However, on this occasion, it was almost a relief to pause
and listen while they absorbed the implications of the
evidence they had just heard.

For his part, Abbot was wondering how Thorne would
react to this outright confirmation that it had been Miranda on the carousel. Surely it must remove any linger-
ing hope the Superintendent might be harbouring. He
was flabbergasted when, as they left the Crawshaws'
house, Thorne said thoughtfully, "Strange the Crawshaws
should have made the same mistake as you, Abbot—
deceived by a yellow suit."

"Er—yes, sir," Abbot managed to mumble.

CHAPTER 5

Back at Headquarters, George Thorne phoned the Chief
Constable's secretary and, on hearing that Midvale was
now back at his desk, asked for an immediate interview.

"Well, I don't know, Superintendent," she said. "It's late
in the afternoon and he's pretty busy."

"It's a personal matter. And very urgent."

"All right, Superintendent. I'll see what I can do."

She was a good secretary and an intelligent woman. She
had recognized the stress in Thorne's voice. "You could
spare him ten minutes, sir, if you would," she said quietly
to the Chief Constable.

Philip Midvale nodded resignedly. It was not really his
job to deal with "personal" problems—even those of senior officers—unless they impinged on discipline. There
was an officer trained to deal with such matters, and he

could call on every possible assistance. The Chief Constable sighed. Detective-Superintendent Thorne had never believed in keeping strictly to the rules.

"Come in," he said as there was a tap at his door. He pointed to the chair opposite his desk. "And sit you down." He smiled. "What can I do for you, Superintendent?"

Thorne didn't return the smile. He gave the Chief Constable a long, calculating look that startled his superior. To cover his surprise, Philip Midvale pushed back his chair and stretched his legs out in front of him. He was a big man, heavily built, whose lazy-seeming body was a cloak for an astute mind. He waited for Thorne to speak.

Thorne pulled hard at his moustache. He liked and respected the Chief, but on this occasion that didn't make it any easier to express himself. "Sir—" he began, and then stopped. Midvale, without making the gesture too obvious, glanced at his watch.

"Sir," Thorne began again, "I know I ought to go through channels, and I'm sorry to approach you direct about this, but I hope you'll understand." He paused. "My —my wife is missing," he said.

"Missing? You mean she's—" No one had yet informed the Chief Constable, who had been out of his office most of the day, of Thorne's report, and he had had little time to consider what his superintendent might want with him. As far as Thorne was concerned, a "missing" wife would have been his last guess.

"I said 'missing' sir, and that's what I meant. She wasn't there when I got home last night, and I've not seen or heard from her since. No note. No phone call. Just—just blank."

"I see. That's not so many hours ago, you know. Could she have had an accident? She drives, of course?"

"Yes, and her car's not in the garage, but . . ."

The Chief Constable listened sympathetically, letting Thorne unburden himself. But he noticed the points that

Thorne didn't make, as well as those he emphasized. It seemed to him that there were one or two unexpected gaps in the Superintendent's account.

"Your wife seemed no different from usual when you parted yesterday morning?" he asked as Thorne came to a stop.

"No different at all, sir. No."

"She was in good spirits, not depressed about anything? Her health?"

"She was fine. There was nothing wrong with her. She's hardly ever ill and, if she had felt sick, she'd have told me."

"And you'd not had a—a tiff, any kind of quarrel?"

"No! We—er—we're not in the habit of quarrelling, sir."

Philip Midvale hesitated. He made a point of learning as much as he thought necessary about the private lives of his staff—especially its senior members—and he was aware that the Thornes' marriage was considered to be surprisingly close and happy, suffering from few of the strains that were endemic in a demanding profession where hours were irregular and dangers sometimes real. Surreptitiously he studied the Superintendent, who was sitting very upright, his face set, his hands gripped together in his lap so tightly that the knuckles shone white. It seemed to him that Thorne's last reply had lacked the assurance of the others. He wondered why, but decided not to pursue the point.

In fact, Thorne was having the greatest difficulty in controlling himself. He knew what the next question would be, and he knew he had to answer it, but also he had to make Midvale understand the reality of his close relationship with his wife if he were to get the kind of immediate but discreet action he wanted. If it became essential in order to find Miranda he'd stand on a dung heap and crow like a cock, but until such a moment arrived he wanted their private life to remain as private as possible.

The silence between the two men lengthened. Then the Chief Constable said, "You said your wife had taken her car, Superintendent? Did she take anything else?"

"Anything else? What do you mean, sir?" Thorne couldn't prevent himself temporizing. "If she was going any distance, or had something cumbersome to carry, she'd naturally take the car, but—"

"Superintendent!" The Chief Constable's patience was becoming exhausted. He had already given Thorne more time than he could spare, and it looked as if the officer was being purposely obtuse. "Pull yourself together, man," he said, "and think! You're a detective. Did your wife take any clothes with her?"

Again Thorne hesitated, staring at his superior. This was it, he thought. Then, "Yes, sir, she did," he said, "with two suitcases and a cosmetic case." He paused. "It looks as if she took everything she might need for— But if you're suggesting that my wife has deliberately gone and left me, sir—left me without any explanation—you're barking up the wrong tree, in spite of all the evidence."

"There's more?"

"Yes, sir," admitted Thorne reluctantly, as he described the results of the afternoon's inquiries. "But with all respect, sir, you haven't understood our situation at all. Miranda would never walk out on me, any more than I'd walk out on her. We don't have that sort of marriage." Even to Thorne the argument sounded weak.

"Maybe not. But surely the fact that her clothes have gone rules out the possibility of a kidnap or an abduction. I've never yet heard of a kidnapper who gave his victim time to pack—and anyway, from what you tell me, your wife was seen to leave alone."

The argument was precisely that which Thorne had expected to encounter. "Some sort of pressure must have been put on her, sir," he said.

"What kind of pressure?" The Chief Constable was clearly sceptical. "Can you suggest anything?"

"No, but—"

The Chief Constable sighed. "What about relations and friends? Have you called any of them?"

Here Thorne was on firmer ground. "Of course, sir," he said at once. "No joy. Anyway, if she went to visit someone, and was suddenly taken ill, say, I'd surely have been contacted. And she never mentioned making any visits, and she would have, if—" Thorne broke off; what was the use of trying to explain the intricacies of his relationship with Miranda? Midvale would never understand.

Behind him Thorne heard the door of the Chief Constable's office open. He stood up. The signal was clear. The interview was over. "Thank you for your time, sir," he added stiffly.

Midvale had been considering the situation. It seemed to him obvious that he was faced with what was known in the trade as a "domestic." But he was no harsh superior. He liked George Thorne, considering him one of his best, most intuitive and experienced officers. And anyway he would have gone out of his way to help any man of his so obviously in distress, but there were limits. The essential work of the Thames Valley Police—as he saw it—had to come first.

He waved to his secretary to shut the door. "I'm sorry, very sorry, Superintendent," he said. "Truly I am. But after what you yourself have learnt today I can't understand how you continue to think that your wife didn't leave of her own free will. And there's no evidence to suggest she's staying away other than voluntarily. Look, George," said the Chief Constable, coming around his desk to be near Thorne, "you know as well as I do that she's not a 'missing person' as such, and with the best will in the world we can't treat her as if she were. I'm sure you don't want to start a public hue and cry that'll alert the news media, and force us to use our limited resources—"

"I understand, sir. Don't think I don't. We're overworked and understaffed," Thorne interrupted, his mouth twisted into a bitter smile. "I've had to make those excuses myself before now."

Midvale hesitated, asking himself if this was deliberate insolence. He decided instead that it was the reaction of a tired man almost at the end of his tether. He said, "Of course you know the facts, Superintendent. There's nothing I can do to alter them. But if you'd like to take a few days off— Call it sick leave, if you like."

"No, thank you, sir. As you say, there's plenty of work to be done."

This time the Chief Constable was in no doubt. Superintendent George Thorne might be down, but he was far from out. Midvale wondered whether to give him some kind of warning, but in the circumstances it was hard to choose the right words.

"Keep me informed of any developments. But let's hope all this'll sort itself out." The Chief Constable tried to sound encouraging. "Maybe she'll be home, or you'll hear from her soon."

"I'll keep you informed, sir," Thorne said coldly as he left his superior's presence.

He went straight to the cloakroom, which was empty. He locked the door of the end cubicle, sat down on the lavatory seat, buried his face in his hands, and fumed. Though he had been half expecting the Chief Constable's reaction, it infuriated him. If Midvale had the kind of marriage in which it was readily accepted that his wife might walk out on him at any time, he, George Thorne, did not.

Then the door of the cloakroom opened, and sighed shut. There were footsteps, the murmur of voices, the noise of urination, running water, the rattle of the metal container as someone pulled out a clean section of towel. Thorne sat still.

"You've heard the latest?" a voice said suddenly; Thorne recognized it as that of a fellow superintendent. "George Thorne's old woman's run off and left him. The poor sod refuses to believe it, and he's running round in small circles trying to prove she's been kidnapped!"

"Another guy, I suppose. Not sure I blame her for getting out. Imagine being married to our George." This was another colleague—an inspector who had never liked Thorne. "Not much fun, in bed or out, I bet."

There was some ribald laughter. The door opened and shut again. Silence. Thorne, alone, found himself shaking. "Damn them! Damn them!" he muttered. The story would be all around Headquarters by now, elaborated by smut and innuendo. They'd be sniggering behind his back, making crude jokes, shitting on his marriage.

To hell with them, Thorne thought savagely. They could do what they liked, say what they liked. He would not give up. He would find Miranda. When she told him to his face that she'd had enough of him he'd believe it, but not before.

CHAPTER 6

The Chief Constable's dinner party on that Tuesday evening was small and informal. As drinks were being served in the Midvales' drawing-room, Sir Leo Farling was taking the opportunity to repeat yet again the story of Jason's death.

"I hope whoever did it gets caught, and gets a good stiff sentence," Mary Band said fiercely. Normally a gentle woman—the wife of Dr. Dick Band, a Colombury general practitioner who was sometimes called upon to act as the local police surgeon—she wasn't apt to express herself with such vehemence. "I can't bear people who hurt children or animals," she added in explanation of her feelings.

"I quite agree with you. Nor can I," Laura Midvale said.

"He's got to be caught first, and at present there don't

seem any signs of that happening." Sir Leo spoke with disgust.

"You mean the good Sergeant Court's not doing his stuff?" Dick Band said, amused.

Sir Leo snorted. "So far he hasn't even managed to discover who bought two great pieces of steak, though you'd think anyone doing that would be remembered, the price of meat these days."

"Darling, he only knew about the steak this morning, and it probably came from some supermarket—" Helen Farling shook her head.

Sir Leo ignored her. "And he can't make anything of the footprints in the field. We've a friend of our daughter staying with us, and he'd stomped all over the place, obliterating any evidence there might have been. You'd think he'd have had more sense."

"That's not fair, darling. After all, it was Stephen who climbed the tree and rescued the meat," Helen protested.

"I know," her husband conceded. "But I still think we should have consulted Philip yesterday, when Jason was killed."

Another guest, a neighbour and a close friend, noted how the Midvales carefully avoided exchanging glances when they heard Sir Leo's remark, and intervened tactfully. "You said your dog was a Dobermann, Sir Leo. I assume he was intended as a guard dog. Are you getting another?"

"I don't know. I suppose we'll have to. Jason was a splendid guard dog, but he was a friend as well—much more than just a pet. We shall miss him on all counts. It's difficult to face the prospect of replacing him immediately."

A good hostess, Laura Midvale was about to change the subject when a maid came in. She was a young, local girl, and her colour heightened as all conversation ceased while everyone looked at her. She addressed herself to the

Chief Constable, her Oxfordshire accent so strong that it wasn't easy to understand her meaning.

"I'm sorry to disturb you, sir, but you're wanted on the telephone," she said. "I told him you had guests, but he wouldn't listen."

"Who, Dora? Did you get his name?" Mrs. Midvale was impatient.

"Yes, ma'am, I think so. It's a Superintendent Thorpe, or Thorne, it sounded like." She stopped, looking helplessly at her employer.

"Thorne!" the Chief Constable said loudly, surprised. He hadn't been expecting such a call, but he reminded himself that he had told the Superintendent to let him know if there were any developments concerning his wife. He hadn't meant the remark to be taken quite so literally, perhaps, but still . . . "If you'll excuse me. This shouldn't take long," he apologized. "When dinner's ready, go in without me. Don't wait, please."

In fact his guests had finished their soup before the Chief Constable returned to them. His face was flushed and his mouth set. He was normally a phlegmatic man, but it was quite obvious that now he was disturbed.

"Trouble?" Sir Leo asked immediately, deciding that it was impossible to ignore Midvale's demeanour.

"Of a sort," Midvale admitted. "One of my senior officers seems to have gone temporarily round the bend. What would anyone think if he came home and found his wife missing, with her car, her clothes and most of her jewellery gone too? Would he insist that she hadn't left him voluntarily, that she must have been abducted? Would any of you?"

"Abducted? Against her will?" There was a murmur of amused dissent. "Whoever heard of a kidnapper giving his victim time to pack?" someone asked.

"Exactly," replied the Chief Constable. "That's what I said to him."

Then Mary Band said, "Philip, are you talking about

George Thorne? Do you mean that Miranda's disappeared? That George doesn't know where she is?"

Sir Leo intervened. "Superintendent Thorne. I know him, too. He's appeared before me as a prosecution witness once or twice. He seemed to me a pretty well-balanced character. But I've never met his wife."

For a moment Philip Midvale was disconcerted. He had forgotten that Thorne's name had been mentioned, and that it would mean something to the Bands, and to Sir Leo. He hesitated, but realized that he was committed. There was no way he could refuse to answer Mary's question.

"Yes," he said. "It's Detective-Superintendent Thorne. His wife, Miranda, seems to have disappeared, though I don't think 'disappeared' is the right word. As far as I can see she's gone away of her own free will—simply walked out on her husband. But Thorne refuses to accept that explanation."

"I don't blame him," Mary Band said at once, and decisively. "It certainly doesn't sound like Miranda. Did she leave George any kind of note?"

"Apparently not," Midvale said.

"That's odd, isn't it?" Mary Band had no hesitation in pursuing the subject. "After all, I do know her—and him," she added. "They seemed to me an ideal couple, and very close."

Confronted with the inquiring faces of his guests, and his wife, Midvale had to concede that "walking out" on her husband was far from what he had been led to expect of Miranda Thorne. What was more, women who did take such a drastic step almost always left some letter; it was husbands who were more likely to vanish without a word. Nevertheless, unless Thorne was lying—and the Chief Constable, who prided himself on being a good judge of character, couldn't believe this—Mrs. Thorne hadn't attempted to explain her action.

Midvale resisted the temptation to curtail the conversation. "There's another point," he admitted finally. "It was why Thorne phoned. Apparently some time ago his wife inherited a few pieces of quite valuable jewellery—of great sentimental as well as monetary value, Thorne said they were. She always kept them separate from the rest of her bits and pieces, because of fear of theft. She tried to hide them, you know—just the sort of thing women will do." He paused, aware that he was sounding a little patronizing. "Anyway, Thorne's just discovered she didn't take these pieces with her, though she took all the rest—even costume stuff."

"From which I take it he argues she didn't depart willingly," Sir Leo Farling said. "Pretty slender evidence, I'd have thought. If she packed in a hurry, she might have forgotten some of her things. As to the lack of a note or letter—" He shrugged. "Maybe she found it too difficult to write immediately if they had been as close as you suggest. I expect he'll hear from her in a day or two."

No one dared to query the Judge's verdict. But, poor George! Mary Band thought. She and Dick would have to do something to help him, though it wouldn't be easy; he would be proud and prickly in such a situation. Her husband's thoughts were running on the same lines.

"Aren't you going to take any action at all?" Dr. Band asked the Chief Constable.

"Oh yes." Midvale had in fact made up his mind in the course of the conversation. "As I said before, I think that the present evidence for an abduction or kidnapping or anything of that kind is minimal. But George Thorne is one of my best officers. We'll do our utmost to help him trace his wife. But no one can make her come back if she doesn't want to do so." With that, he resolutely turned the conversation to other matters. With a flash of inspiration, he asked after Sir Leo's orchids.

Behind the house where Jean Haule lived, a shed stood in a small, untidy garden. In the past it had contained a few gardening tools and a quantity of junk, but when they had first arrived Willie Burwash had suggested that he and Bert should clean it out and use it as a kind of private hideaway.

Jean had hesitated, distrusting their need for such a retreat, but in the end they had convinced her. After all, the house was small for three adults and two young teen-agers. When the kids came home from school she would want them to do their homework in peace, without Bert and Willie boozing and smoking, not to mention the noise of the TV they would inevitably be watching. Besides, she couldn't imagine any devilment they could concoct in the shed that they couldn't equally well plan in the house or the local pub.

It had proved an admirable—and amicable—arrangement. The shed was cleared and cleaned. A couple of chairs and a table were found, together with a paraffin stove for warmth and a lamp for light. "Bert and I can always play cards there," Willie had said.

"It'll be a home from home," Bert had agreed.

"We might even put up a curtain at the window," Willie added.

And so they had, to Jean's surprise. In a way, the curtain re-aroused her doubts but, after one or two unexpected visits when she had found them merely listening to the radio, yarning and indeed in the middle of a game of pontoon, her suspicions had evaporated. Now she was thankful that Willie had suggested turning the shed into what was effectively an extra room.

On that Tuesday evening, while the Midvales were entertaining their dinner guests, Bert Parker and Willie Burwash, having had their own supper, retreated to their hideout. Bert lit the stove and the lamp, and Willie unearthed a long brown paper parcel that had been carefully hidden in a corner behind some deck-chairs.

Before he put it on the table, he double-checked that the key was turned in the lock and the curtain completely drawn; the young Haules could be just as curious as Jean. Then, assured that they would have warning of any interruption, he unwrapped the parcel. Tenderly he removed layers of newspaper and sacking, until the shotgun was revealed.

"There!" he said. "She's a beauty, isn't she?"

Bert nodded, though he wasn't particularly keen on shooters of any kind. "Did Eddie Mull want to know why you wanted it?" he asked.

"No. He knew we were pals of brother Tony, and we'd done what we could for him when we were all inside together. That was enough."

"But he'll expect to be paid sometime. I wasn't thinking of a brand-new effort. That gun cost money," Bert said. "Unless it fell off the back of a lorry, of course."

"He didn't ask any questions. And nor did I," Willie said shortly.

Bert lit a cigarette and pushed the packet across the table to Willie. "If Jean finds out—" he said.

"She won't."

"What do we tell her? She's bound to hear us when we go out tonight."

"We'll be quiet."

"The bloody house is made of cardboard."

"We'll say we're going to try and snare a few rabbits."

"D'you think she'll believe that? She's no fool, my sister, you know."

"I know, Bert. But not to worry. We might even get a bunny, and she won't complain about that. It can be a contribution to the week's housekeeping." He grinned as he began to wrap up the shotgun.

George Thorne had found the pieces of jewellery, which Miranda had inherited from an aunt and of which she was so fond, in their hiding place at the bottom of an old workbasket on the top shelf of the cupboard above Miranda's wardrobe. The discovery had filled him with momen-

tary elation. Here was proof positive that Miranda hadn't
left him of her own free will. She would never have forgotten these pieces or left them behind—particularly the
diamond pendant that could be detached and used as a
brooch, which was a special favourite of hers.

That the Chief Constable hadn't received this information with equal enthusiasm didn't worry Thorne. Whatever Midvale's reaction, it remained a solid factor that
must be taken into account, the Superintendent told himself. Now, at last, there must be action—real action—action of a kind he understood and could control. Perhaps
he should have been more insistent earlier, but . . .

His exhilaration faded as he sank into his favourite chair
and realized the position into which his logic had forced
him. Desertion or abduction—what a choice! But the fact
must be faced that abduction was preferable, though the
thought of Miranda in the hands of kidnappers was un-
bearable. But at least if she'd been kidnapped there was a
chance—a detective's chance—of recovering his wife,
whereas if she had left him voluntarily . . .

Exhaustion was beginning to take its toll on George
Thorne. He found his eyes growing heavy. He drowsed,
then slept. When he woke he felt stiff, but he rose to his
feet and shook himself impatiently. This was no time for
snoozing—it must be bed first, and then hard, determined
effort in the morning.

He went into the kitchen in search of the whisky bottle
but, remembering his recent hangover, decided against
it. Instead he made himself some tea, weak as he liked it,
with a slice of lemon. It was the end of the lemon, and
because he had left it on the draining-board it was slightly
mouldy, and he had to scrape off the bad part before
slicing it.

Thorne was a fastidious man, and this action made him
wrinkle his nose in disgust. It also had the effect of making
him glance around. He saw the dirty dishes, the burnt
frying-pan still soaking in the sink, the fat spilt on top of

the stove. It was the same in the sitting-room, flowers dead, plants beginning to wilt, dust on smooth surfaces, and he knew that upstairs his bed was unmade, merely pulled together roughly.

Miranda, he thought, would be ashamed of the state he had allowed their house to get into in such a short time. He would have to do something about it, and about food. If she returned home—hurriedly he corrected this in his mind to *when* she returned home—he must have the place looking as if she had just left it.

Thorne sat at the kitchen table with his tea. He would have liked one of Miranda's homemade biscuits, but the tin was empty. Tomorrow he must do a little shopping, he thought, though at the back of his mind he knew perfectly well that this kind of activity would merely serve to conceal his real concern.

The telephone rang. By now the sound no longer made Thorne's stomach lurch with anticipation, but it was late in the evening and he wasn't expecting a call. He hurried to the instrument.

"Hello," he said cautiously, and gave his number.

For a minute there was no response, but he could hear music in the background and he was conscious of someone at the other end of the line.

"Who's that?" he demanded finally.

"Miranda."

"Darling!" He could hardly believe it, but it was Miranda's voice, rather low-pitched for a woman, and soft; it was unmistakable, though the line was poor, and the background music—just like that in the other mysterious call yesterday evening—didn't help.

"Darling," he repeated. "Where are you? Are you all right?"

"Yes. George, I'm not coming back. This is goodbye."

"But, Miranda—darling—"

"Goodbye, George."

The line went dead.

Thorne gripped the receiver with all his strength. His first thought was disbelief, in spite of the unmistakable voice. Then he was kicking himself for not having made arrangements to tap his phone and trace any such calls. But how could he have set such a complex operation in motion, in the face of the Chief Constable's scepticism?

Slowly and reluctantly Thorne put the receiver back on its rest, thereby severing, or so it seemed to him, the last link with his wife.

But why? he asked himself. Why? There had to be a reason. He remembered each of the few words she had spoken, and now they struck him as false, like those of a poor actress with badly scripted lines.

As he walked back to the kitchen and his tea, Thorne's stooping shoulders suddenly straightened. Of course, he thought, he should have known at once. This case was so close to home that his judgement was affected. Miranda had been compelled to make that call, or it was so brief and stilted it could have been a doctored tape. Whatever the Chief Constable might or might not believe, he knew his Miranda. She hadn't left him willingly.

CHAPTER 7

Stephen Crispin woke with a start and sat up in bed. He strained to listen. The curtains were drawn back, allowing moonlight to filter through the clouds and make deep shadows around the furniture in Lucy's bedroom. It was still night—the early hours of Wednesday morning, according to his watch. He could hear the faintest rustle of the creeper growing outside the open window, but nothing else.

"Stephen, what is it?"

Lucy sat up beside him. Like Stephen she was naked,

and she made no effort to cover her small, high breasts. Automatically he put out a hand to her.

"What is it?" she repeated. "Do you want to make love again?"

"No." Stephen withdrew his hand somewhat reluctantly. "Contain yourself, woman. Don't be so eager." He laughed. "I thought I heard something. A strange sort of noise. Funny. I can't quite describe it."

"Try? After all, you're meant to be a novelist."

"It sounded like heavy gravel or very fine pebbles being thrown at glass."

"Sounds odd to me," said Lucy. "Perhaps you dreamt it."

"No. There it is again. Didn't you hear it?"

"Ye-es. It sounded a bit like buckshot. There was a soft bang first. Someone potting rabbits, perhaps."

"At this time of night?"

Lucy had no chance to answer. Immediately there came the sound of breaking glass, as if a window had been shattered, by a cricket ball, say. The noise acted on Stephen like a trigger. He threw back the bedclothes and leapt out of bed.

"What on earth are you doing? It was probably just a cat. No burglar worth his salt would make as much noise as that." Lucy was scornful. "Anyway, even if we've got a burglar Carter'll be after him. He's sleeping downstairs at the moment, till Dad can replace poor Jason."

Stephen Crispin was trying to find his pyjamas. Lucy was not the tidiest of girls, and the bedroom carpet seemed to be littered with clothes of both sexes. But at last he found them, and climbed into the trousers, in his haste staggering first on one leg, then the other.

"I must go."

"Why? Darling, I love you dearly, but I don't see you as the heroic type—anti-hero more. And if there's anything, Carter'll deal with it. He's more than just a houseman, you know. Dad had him, and our chauffeur, trained in judo and that sort of stuff."

"It's not that. I'm no hero, anti- or otherwise." Stephen was now in his pyjamas and was struggling into his dressing-gown. "Don't you realize? All this excitement may well have woken your parents. If the house is going to be roused, you don't want me to be found in here, do you?"

"Oh, Stephen!" Lucy hooted with laughter. "Do you think Mum and Dad don't guess we sleep together? Dad doesn't approve, I'm sure, but I told Mum we'd be getting married soon, and she'll have passed on the happy news."

"Married?" Stephen was distracted from his immediate preoccupations. His voice came out as a squeak. "But—"

"Think about it. You'll soon get used to the idea. It would please Dad enormously. He's yearning for grandchildren."

"But why me? I've no money. I'm not in the same league as you." He waved his hands helplessly, as if to include in the gesture the Manor and the entire possessions of the Farlings.

"Darling, for a modern novelist you're awfully old-fashioned. Dad'll increase my allowance. We'll get by. As to why you?" Lucy contemplated him for a moment, her head bent to one side. "I'm tired of public school idiots, and one of these days you'll be famous. You'll probably win the Booker next year, or the year after, or the year after that. Besides—" She patted the bed beside her suggestively. "You're very good here."

"Not now," Stephen Crispin said firmly. "If I'm to be the Judge's son-in-law—and I doubt if he's all that keen on the idea—he's not going to catch me in your bed."

"Okay. We'll save it for—"

Lucy ceased abruptly. Stephen had opened the bedroom door, and they both heard it. This time the noise came from inside the house, and it sounded like a heavy thump.

"Carter!" said Lucy. "He must have bumped into a bit

of furniture. Be careful he doesn't take you for an intruder."

Stephen grunted. He had no wish to get involved with
any intruders—or with Carter. In spite of Lucy's equa-
nimity, he remained embarrassed at the thought of his last
midnight encounter with the houseman the previous
night. He felt in the pocket of his dressing-gown for the
torch that Lucy had produced to assist him this time,
waved to her and shut the bedroom door behind him.

Alone in the dark corridor Stephen paused and listened.
There were the usual creaks and groans of an old house,
but nothing identifiable or untoward. He switched on the
torch and, keeping the beam directed to the floor, set off
for his own room. If the Farlings were as happy about him
and Lucy as she thought, he reflected uncharitably, they
might have made things more convenient for him, and
not put him at the further end of the house. Wary of
meeting Carter, he moved slowly and cautiously, careful
to make no noise.

As it emerged, he need hardly have bothered. He had
just reached the gallery along the top of the wide curving
staircase when the show commenced.

First he heard footsteps—soft, but pounding—people
running, he thought at once. A door was flung back violently, presumably against a wall, and there was a muffled
shout. He could see nothing, but he had the impression of
shadowy shapes in the broad hall below. Then the lights
came on, blinding with their brightness.

Involuntarily, Stephen Crispin took a step backwards.
The next moment, driven by curiosity rather than hero-
ism or any desire to intervene, he was leaning on the
balustrade, gazing down. He was in time to see two dark
figures running in the direction of the drawing-room.
Both wore black track suits with stocking masks over their
heads. And—it really was too close to farce to be true—
each seemed to be carrying a sack, presumably of loot,
Stephen thought at once.

As they reached the middle of the hall, Carter appeared from a door outside Stephen's line of vision. He was wearing slacks and a sweater; clearly he hadn't been suddenly woken from sleep, but had been on patrol around the house. In his hand was what Stephen took to be a heavy truncheon and, as Stephen watched, he threw it expertly at the slighter of the two figures, who was some yards behind the other.

It landed between the shoulder-blades of the fleeing thief, who fell forwards, dropping a sack. Bits of silver rolled out of it across the carpet. And suddenly Carter leapt. In almost one movement he reclaimed his truncheon and pulled the stocking mask from his quarry's face.

Perhaps he was as surprised as Stephen Crispin to see what was revealed—the face of a woman with pointed features and short reddish hair. Perhaps he was just careless and, in the heat of the moment, had forgotten her companion. But, as he straightened, there was a sharp report.

Carter dropped the truncheon and clasped his chest. Then slowly his legs gave way, and he sank to the ground. Meanwhile, the woman—now from her shape so obviously female—had scrambled to her feet and was running for the drawing-room door. The man who had fired the shot waited for her to get clear.

The whole scene—from farce to drama, if not tragedy— had taken place with such speed that only a matter of seconds had elapsed between Stephen Crispin's arrival at the gallery above and Carter's collapse on the hall floor below. Crispin had watched the sequence of events, eyes wide, mouth slightly open, like a child watching an exciting film. The unreality of the scene was such that he had made no attempt to take part, not even to shout a warning to Carter, though in retrospect he realized that he had seen the gun being levelled at the houseman. He had stood, motionless and mesmerized. It was not until the man with the gun turned to follow the woman that Crispin moved.

It was a mistake. The slight movement must have caught the gunman's eye. He stopped, took aim and fired. Crispin dropped his torch and ducked. In fact, he was in no real danger. It was a difficult snap shot, and ricocheted harmlessly off the balustrade. But it left its target trembling.

By now, however, there had been enough noise to waken others. Doors were opening. Crispin heard Sir Leo's voice. Lucy was calling, too. He could hardly just stand there in the corridor. The man with the gun had disappeared, so he took his courage in both hands and ran down the stairs to kneel beside the still figure.

Carter had fallen sideways and rolled on to his back. His sweater was dark in colour, but at close quarters it was possible to see an even darker, spreading stain. His face was ashen, and he showed no signs of respiration. Crispin touched him tentatively, then flinched as he realized his hand had become sticky with blood.

Crispin rose slowly to his feet, breathing shallowly and staggering slightly as the full significance of what had happened hit him.

"Stephen! Are you all right?"

Lucy was the first to reach him and support him. She was closely followed by Sir Leo and Helen. Crispin hesitated.

"Yes, I'm all right," he said finally. "But I—I think that Carter's dead."

"Carter!" cried Lady Farling. "Oh no! Not dead! Not Carter! It's impossible." She was shocked out of her natural calm.

Sir Leo's reaction was more practical. "Helen, ring Band—and tell him we need an ambulance," he ordered at once. He turned to Crispin. "What happened?" he demanded.

Crispin shrugged. "I don't really know. I heard noises.

There were people running. The lights came on. Carter was chasing two characters in black track suits. Thieves, I assumed. I'd just reached the top of the stairs when one of them turned round and shot him. Then—then he fired at me."

"But you're all right?" Lucy repeated.

"Yes. He missed."

Sir Leo issued more orders. He would call the police. Nothing must be touched, especially not the open French window in the drawing-room which could well have been the intruders' point of entry. Helen was to turn up the central heating, and find brandy in the library. Lucy and Crispin should go to the kitchen and make tea.

By the time they all reassembled Stephen Crispin had recovered most of his composure, though he was still dazed. It had been an extraordinary night. Lucy had proposed to him; he had seen a man killed; he himself had been shot at; and, what was more, he seemed to have come out of the whole episode with credit. No one had questioned his presence at the top of the stairs; instead the Farlings seemed to be treating him like a minor hero.

Two large brandies later Crispin had begun to believe that perhaps he had acted rather sensibly and, as he went upstairs to dress before the police arrived, he felt elated, as well as slightly drunk. He pulled on his clothes quickly and went downstairs.

The library now seemed to be full of people, as well as the three Farlings, and all of them turned to Crispin as he entered the room. Sir Leo made hasty introductions. Dr. Band, who had briefly examined the body; Sergeant Court from Colombury; and another uniformed police officer.

"Ah, you'll be the chief witness then," Court said. "You saw the whole incident, Mr. Crispin."

"Not the whole of it," Stephen Crispin objected.

"But you saw the actual shooting."

"Yes," Crispin agreed. "I suppose you'll want me to make a statement?" he said.

"No. Not yet, sir. I've been in touch with Thames Valley Headquarters. Officers from the Serious Crime Squad will be on their way by now. This is a very serious crime, you know, sir—murder during an attempted robbery."

"Who will they send?" interrupted Sir Leo.

"I don't know, sir. But it could be Detective-Superintendent Thorne, if he's free—and considering that you know him, sir."

"I see," said Sir Leo shortly. He wasn't enthusiastic. Remembering the Superintendent's current marital problem, he would have preferred that someone else— someone less involved in his own domestic affairs—should be allocated to the case.

Will Burwash was driving fast, Bert Parker beside him. They had "borrowed" a car from an elderly couple who lived at the furthest end of Jean's row of council houses, and they intended to return it before it was missed. They knew the couple would never notice that the car had done a few extra miles.

They hadn't spoken since they got into the car. Parker kept gingerly feeling his throat; if he had been wearing a shirt he would have loosened the collar. He swallowed and coughed several times.

"For God's sake stop making those bleeding noises!" Burwash said.

"It's all right for you." Parker had difficulty speaking. "It wasn't you he half throttled."

"Maybe not. But you'll survive." Burwash showed no sign of sympathy.

Parker grunted in disgust. "Of all the fucking luck," he said, "to run into them like that."

"There's no harm done, or none to come, providing we both keep our traps shut. You're not thinking of squealing, are you, Bert?"

"Don't be a bloody fool. He said he'd do us if we so

much as gave a wink in their direction, and he wasn't kidding."

"Eddie never kids," Burwash said. Then suddenly he laughed aloud. "Cheer up, Bert. It's been a good night's work all around, if you ask me. That sodding old judge isn't going to forget it in a hurry."

He hooted indignantly as an approaching car passed them going very fast. He couldn't know that it was an unmarked police car, driven by Sergeant Abbot, or that the man beside the driver was Superintendent Thorne.

CHAPTER 8

A few hours later the full panoply of a major police operation had been deployed. A mobile incident van was parked in the drive of the Manor; an ambulance stood beside it, ready to remove Carter's body after the pathologist, who was expected shortly from Oxford, had examined it *in situ*. Meanwhile, the scene of crime team was busy in the house.

All the main protagonists had had preliminary interviews with Detective-Superintendent Thorne, and they remained wide awake as they now sat in a semicircle in the library, facing him. Neither Sir Leo nor Lady Farling had slept at all, though Lucy and Stephen Crispin had managed to doze in short snatches. As was only to be expected, Carter's death, the burglary and the subsequent invasion by the authorities had all combined to prevent any attempt at real rest.

Thorne himself had been roused from a terrifying nightmare in which Miranda was about to be shot by a firing-squad unless he—her husband—obeyed some instructions he failed to comprehend. In fact, he was probably more weary than anyone else, for in the circumstances even the prospect of a murder inquiry had failed to force adrenalin through his body. But no one except Sergeant Abbot, sitting apart with his notebook on his knees, would have guessed this. Thorne managed to sound efficient and businesslike, as if his mind were wholly concentrated on the job in hand. The only thing that might have revealed his preoccupation was an unaccustomed, slightly pedantic turn of phrase, and even this might have been induced by the fact that he was facing a judge.

"It would appear to be a straightforward crime," he said, "and you must forgive me if I reiterate what you all know, and ask questions you have been asked before. I assure you they have a purpose." To himself he added, wearily, "I hope they do."

Sir Leo's reply was equally formal. "Providing you get the villains you can ask or do what you like," he said gruffly. "Naturally we'll cooperate."

Helen Farling intervened suddenly. "I wish you wouldn't all take it so calmly," she said. "After all, it was Carter—Carter—who's been killed."

Thorne acknowledged this contribution with a small nod of his head. "I know, Lady Farling, and I'm sorry," he remarked. "But Sir Leo's right: the thing to do now is trace those who killed him. And by this time we know a great deal. We know that two unauthorized persons"— Abbot raised his eyebrows at this incredibly ponderous phrase—"entered this house by forcing one of the French windows in the drawing-room. We know they went to the dining-room, where they were collecting silver and other valuable objects when they were interrupted by the houseman, Robert Carter. We know that Carter was deliberately fired upon—with fatal results—by one of the intruders, apparently in order to prevent him from capturing the other. We have a stocking mask and a sack. We don't have the weapon, but we have two rounds fired from it. And we know the exact time of the shooting. We also have some kind of description of the intruders. As I said, it's a great deal."

"It's a hell of a lot," Lucy said. "Surely with all that you can't fail to find them."

"Possibly not, Miss Farling, but this crime has all the hallmarks of professionalism, and that means it could be difficult to prove guilt in a court." Thorne smiled thinly. "I'm sure Sir Leo will understand what I mean."

Sir Leo nodded. "Professional criminals take care to cover their tracks and arrange alibis and so on," he said curtly. Then, addressing the Superintendent, "Have you looked outside the house yet?"

Thorne shook his head. "Only cursorily so far. There was no point in officers stumbling around in the dark or under floodlights destroying evidence. But it's getting light now and my men will be starting the search. Meanwhile, I'd like some background. Tell me more about your household, sir."

"If you mean how it's run, that's my job," Helen Farling said. "This isn't a big house for a manor, fortunately, and Sir Leo and I live very simply. Inside, Carter was able to cope, with the help of two girls from Colombury who come in daily. I do the cooking myself, unless we have visitors or there's some emergency, when I depend on Mrs. Wain. Wain himself is our gardener and odd job man. He and his wife live in the village. So does Sir Leo's chauffeur—his name's Dale, Reginald Dale."

This was not exactly Thorne's idea of a simple lifestyle, but he had met with others much grander and more exotic. "Thank you, Lady Farling, that's most helpful," he said. "So there were five people actually sleeping in the house last night. Or, to be more precise, four sleeping— and Carter, fully dressed and on guard duty. Did he usually wander round the house in the small hours?"

"Sometimes," Sir Leo said. "He told us he suffered from occasional insomnia. But of course there'd have been no need for guard duty, as you call it, if Jason were with us. If anyone had got in while that dog was alive, he'd have regretted it. Poisoning Jason is one of the things I'll never forgive this scum for." He forestalled his wife's protest by adding, "Apart from Carter, of course."

"Sergeant Court told me about the Dobermann, sir. If we assume there's a connection between the dog's death and tonight's events, it confirms my belief that this job was planned carefully, professionally—and with inside help."

"What?"

"But that's not possible."

"Are you suggesting—"

There was an explosion of disagreement from the Farlings and Thorne said, "Doesn't it strike you as odd that the intruders seem to have been so familiar with the house?" He didn't wait for any answers, but continued on a different track. "Now, I know it's going over the same ground twice, but I'd like to get the sequence of events quite clear in my mind. I want you to show me, at the same time as you describe your actions, what each of you heard and did. It might refresh your memories, and you might recall some little thing that could turn out to be important."

"I thought reconstruction of crimes only happened in French movies," Lucy murmured *sotto voce* to Crispin as Thorne led the way out of the library into the hall.

The pieces of silver and *objets d'art* left scattered on the floor had been photographed, fingerprinted and carefully collected, but Carter's body remained, a sheet-covered mound with a police officer standing nearby. Helen Farling stared at it pityingly, then averted her eyes.

"Poor Carter!" she said. "It was such a—a stupid way to die. None of the things were worth his life."

Thorne said gently, "According to Dr. Band, he died almost instantaneously, Lady Farling. At least he didn't suffer."

Helen sighed. "That's a good thing. But can't you—now—"

"I'm afraid the body can't be moved till the pathologist has examined it here, Lady Farling." Thorne anticipated her question, and shepherded them up the stairs, Abbot following. The Superintendent turned to Stephen Crispin. "You were the first on the scene, Mr. Crispin. You heard some noise and came out of your room and along the corridor in time to see the actual shooting. Indeed, you're the only witness to it."

"Er—yes." Crispin glanced at Lucy; he knew he was placing himself in a false position, but could see no way of avoiding it without admitting that in reality he had been quietly leaving Lucy's bed.

"But everything happened very quickly," he added. "Almost as soon as I got to the top of the stairs, the lights came on, as I told you."

He began to recount what he had seen, this time in more detail, though Thorne's repeated demands for precision worried him. He could visualize the scene fairly clearly, but he found it hard to be exact. His head had started to ache, and he wished he'd not had that second brandy.

"Thank you, Mr. Crispin," Thorne said. "Now, show me just where you were standing when Carter turned the lights on—presumably it was Carter."

"That would be correct, Superintendent," Sir Leo intervened. "There are switches for the hall lights just beside the door from the dining-room."

Crispin had moved a yard or so to his right. "I was about here," he said. "I stepped back without thinking, and then forward again."

"You saw the woman's face when the stocking was pulled off. Can't you describe her more fully?" Thorne asked.

"Not really."

"But you know she was a woman. How can you be

certain, if you can't describe her?" Thorne was growing impatient.

"Well, she seemed the right shape and—" Crispin groped for words. "Her face looked very pale and pointed and white," he said at last.

"Would you recognize her again, Mr. Crispin? Could you identify her in a line of suspects, for instance?"

"I don't know, Superintendent. I doubt it."

Thorne stifled his irritation. To have a direct witness—a witness who might have been expected to be intelligent and observant—and to find him so vague was bloody annoying. He turned to Lucy Farling. "You were next on the scene, Miss Farling. Presumably you were woken by the commotion?"

"No. I sleep at the other end of the house. I might not have heard anything, but I was awake." Lucy smiled cheerfully at Crispin, who ignored her. "I'd been woken before, by someone potting rabbits, and then the sound of breaking glass. Did the thieves break a window?"

"Potting rabbits, Miss Farling?" Thorne said. "And breaking glass? That's new. I've not been told that any windows—"

Sir Leo interrupted. "Good God, girl, why didn't you tell us before? The greenhouses are near your windows. Buckshot, Superintendent! Broken glass! Come on!"

Sir Leo was already running down the stairs, closely followed by his wife. Lucy followed, crying that she was sorry, but she hadn't thought. Crispin, who had no idea what was happening, but had no desire to be left alone with the police officers, went after them.

"What the—" Thorne said, making no effort to move.

"It'll be the Judge's orchids he's fearful about," Abbot explained. "He's got a lot of rare species, I've heard, and if someone's peppered his greenhouses all the heat'll be escaping, and the orchids won't like that."

"I see. But—but if you're going to burgle a house, why

announce your presence first? And—" He gestured at Carter's body. "That wasn't done by any shotgun."

"The Judge seems more interested in his dog and his orchids than in a murder in his own front hall," commented Superintendent Thorne, oddly acerbic. "It doesn't make sense," he added, almost at random, "unless of course there's no connection, and we've got two separate incidents on our hands. That would be an awful coincidence. I don't like coincidences."

"They happen more often than one cares to think, sir," said the detective-inspector in charge of the scene-of-crime team.

It was full daylight now, and they were standing in the garden of the Manor, Sergeant Abbot a respectful step to one side and all three gazing in the direction of the greenhouses. They could see the figures of Sir Leo and his gardener moving anxiously among the orchids; fortunately only one of the houses had been riddled with shot, so that it had been possible to move most of the plants and the damage was less than might have been expected. Lady Farling, having checked the list of items that were missing, had gone to catch up on lost sleep, while Lucy and Stephen Crispin had been told they could return to Oxford, as long as they stayed readily available. The police investigation continued.

Nearby an officer was cordoning off a small plot of ground around some shrubs, and another was making a cast of a shoe-print. Thorne regarded them morosely. There was ample evidence to show that two individuals— at least one of them a man, to judge by his shoe size—had stood there and taken a pot with a shotgun at Sir Leo's greenhouses. At the same time, it seemed that two others were busy breaking into the house. It was ludicrous, Thorne decided, absolutely ludicrous—but everything these days was mad; for a moment his thoughts returned to his own affairs.

"I'll leave it to you then, Inspector," he said heavily. "Time I went and had a word with the staff. They should all have arrived by now."

"Formal interviews, sir?" Abbot asked as they walked back towards the house. "Or chat-ups?"

"Half and half," Thorne said. "Sir Leo says we can use the library. We'll start with the indoor help. What about this Mrs. Wain? She only comes in when she's asked, doesn't she?"

"I've made sure she's available, sir," Abbot said eagerly. Lady Farling and her daughter had provided only a sketchy breakfast, and he was hungry. Previously he had always been able to rely on the Superintendent to ensure that they had regular meals, but since his wife had gone, Thorne had become uninterested in food. Abbot could sympathize, but he had hopes that the part-time cook might produce some early elevenses.

Eventually his hopes were justified. Mrs. Wain promised to organize some food. Otherwise she was no help, for she had spent the night at home in the village with her husband, until they had both been summoned to the Manor. She volunteered that the Farlings were excellent employers and well liked; everyone would be most upset by what had occurred. But that was all. She had seen no one around the Manor who was not entitled to be there; she had heard of no one making inquiries in the village about the Farlings or their house; except for poor Jason's death, she could think of nothing unusual that had happened recently.

Grace Davis—a cheerful but plain-looking girl who brought in a tray with a large jug of coffee, a plate of hot buttered toast and some scones—had even less to offer, as she lived further away, in Colombury. She had noticed no strangers around the place nor anything untoward, nor anyone asking unusual questions.

Nor, apparently, had Joyce Greene, the other daily girl from Colombury, though there the resemblance ended.

First, Joyce Greene was an extremely pretty girl, with an attractive figure, fair hair and large brown eyes, which most of the time she kept demurely cast down. Then, she answered "yes" or "no" to most of Thorne's questions, rarely producing a comment of her own accord. When Thorne said she might go, her relief was obvious.

"And what did you think of her, Sergeant?" Thorne asked when the door had shut.

On some other occasion Bill Abbot might have given an honest answer, but he knew that at present the Superintendent was in no mood to appreciate a ribald comment. Instead, he said seriously, "She was nervous, sir, yet she didn't strike me as a normally nervous type—quite the reverse at the local disco, perhaps."

Thorne nodded his agreement. "And why should she be nervous, one wonders? She's got something on her conscience, that one, though it probably isn't relevant." He drained his coffee cup, and looked to see if Abbot had finished eating. "We'll leave it for now, anyway, and go and talk to the chauffeur. Though he doesn't sleep here, either," he added.

They found Reg Dale furiously cleaning Sir Leo's car. He had, he said, been a mate of Carter's. He was angry, as well as upset, at his friend's death, and he had no hesitation in speaking his mind. "It was so bloody pointless—the killing, I mean. There's too much damned violence these days. Okay. I can understand them wanting to nick the stuff. Maybe they're on the dole, and no prospect of getting off it. They see others living well, and—" He shrugged. "But that gives them no call to shoot Bob Carter."

Thorne let Dale talk out his anger, then started on his questions. He got no more from the chauffeur than he had from Mrs. Wain and the two girls, but as they were about to leave Dale returned to his theme.

"And the vandalism! All this blasted vandalism! I don't

know what people get out of it. The glasshouse! And take
what they did to Lady Farling's car the other month—"
"And what was that?" Thorne inquired casually.
"Don't you know?" The chauffeur was surprised. "It
was reported to the police."
"A different department, maybe. We've not heard of it.
Tell us."
"Sure, but it was at least a month ago, so it can't be
connected with this business, can it?" When Thorne failed
to answer, Dale shook his head in incomprehension, but
continued the story. "It happened in Oxford. Lady
Farling left her car in Broad Street. A nice public place,
you'd think. But when she came back there were deep
scratches on both sides—looked as if they'd been made by
a knife—and the door had been forced, and red paint
sprayed all over the upholstery. Absolute bloody wanton
damage!"
"What was Lady Farling driving? Was it a distinctive
car?"
The chauffeur stared at Thorne. "I know what you're
thinking, Superintendent. A judge and his family are always at risk from villains he's sent down—and, sure, no
other cars were touched on this occasion, as far as I know.
But it was only a brown Ford Escort. There are thousands
of them on the road. It could easily have been chance."
He paused. "Unless they knew the licence number, of
course," he added thoughtfully.
That was the sum total of Dale's contribution, and the
two detectives went off to the greenhouses, where Sir Leo
and his gardener were busy with the orchids. They made
it clear they had little time for interruptions or questions,
but Thorne persevered and eventually elicited from Sir
Leo the tale of the lighted cigar that had been slipped into
his pocket as he walked through St. Giles' Fair on Monday
afternoon.
"Lady Farling's car, the cigar or cigarillo, the attack on
the orchid house—they all fit," Thorne said, as Abbot

drove them back to Kidlington. "Perhaps too neatly. No one could have known Sir Leo was going to take that route through the Fair. But armed robbery, preceded by the poisoning of the guard dog; that's a different kettle of fish." He shook his head slowly.

For the rest of the journey, concentrated on the case, he scarcely spoke, and it wasn't until they were approaching their Headquarters that he realized he hadn't given a thought to Miranda for several hours.

CHAPTER 9

Once back at his Kidlington Headquarters, Detective-Superintendent Thorne was immediately beset by inquiries —phone calls, demands that he should take this or that action, requests for meetings. The rape case which had been the cause of his presence in the centre of Oxford on Monday afternoon had resolved itself; the suspect, his alibi broken, had simply confessed. There was, however, to be an inquiry into the death of Jack Taylor, the youth who had hanged himself in his cell a couple of months ago, and there were the usual vociferous demands that it should be held in public. Thorne shuddered at the paperwork all this would involve. Naturally, the Chief Constable wanted to see him about the Farling case, and a woman called Iris Grayson, of whom he had never heard, had left a message asking him to telephone her urgently.

Thorne instructed Abbot to check on any recently released prisoners who might have a grudge against Sir Leo, and to check the Farlings' staff and their house guest Stephen Crispin through central records. Then he went along to the Chief Constable's office and made his report. Midvale was glad to see that though Thorne didn't look at his best, he seemed to be concentrating on his work.

"A peculiar kind of case," Midvale summed up. "It's already led to a killing—so that's what matters now, Superintendent—but it's odd. The robbery and the shooting, which I suppose was unpremeditated, don't seem to me to tie up with the rest, except perhaps for the poisoning of the guard dog."

"I tend to agree, sir. The cigar affair, the vandalism to Lady Farling's car and the glasshouse business—they seem to be on a different scale, somehow. Petty revenge, perhaps, but the other—" Thorne shook his head.

Midvale sighed. "The main thing is to get results—and soon, too. Sir Leo's a personal friend, and he'll expect quick action." He waited till Thorne was at the door before he said, "Any news of your wife yet?"

"No, sir."

The Superintendent shut the door firmly behind him; he would not again discuss Miranda with the Chief Constable. He went along to the canteen, ate a rapid tasteless meal, and returned to his office. Mrs. Iris Grayson had phoned once more. Please would Mr. Thorne call back as soon as possible; it was a personal matter.

Thorne might have ignored these requests from someone he had never to his knowledge heard of, except for the word "personal." He tapped out her number, wondering if by any chance he ought to be able to identify Mrs. Grayson.

"Superintendent Thorne? Oh, how kind of you to phone." It was a pleasant voice. "I'm sorry to bother you like this, but I've tried over and over and there's no answer from your home, and I'm terribly worried about Miranda. She's usually so reliable. She's never let me down before without any warning. So when she didn't come and I heard nothing, I knew something must be badly wrong."

As Mrs. Grayson paused for breath, George Thorne found himself gripping the receiver tightly. He swallowed hard, and had to make an effort to keep his voice level.

"Mrs. Grayson, I'm sorry, but I don't understand. What did you expect Miranda to do for you?"

"Ah, how stupid of me! I should have explained, but I thought Miranda might have mentioned me. I'm the Meals on Wheels lady who goes out with your wife. Our day is Tuesday, but yesterday she didn't come, and there was no message, no nothing. It's not like her, as I said. She's never let me down before. She's one of the most conscientious of helpers. I do hope she's not ill."

"No, but there's illness in the family," Thorne lied glibly. "She was called away very suddenly. I'm sorry, Mrs. Grayson. I remember she did ask me to phone you, but—"

He had to listen to a few minutes of sympathy and understanding, but he didn't mind. Mrs. Grayson's assessment of Miranda's virtues had added to his small store of hope, and he had been forced to admit that hope was dwindling. As Iris Grayson talked, George Thorne reflected. Today was Wednesday; surely if Miranda were being held against her will as a hostage of some kind he would have received a threat, a demand, by now. What he needed was a lead . . .

As if in answer to this unspoken wish there was a knock at the door as he finally put down the receiver, and Sergeant Abbot came in. "Sir, I may have news for you. About your wife's car."

"Has it been found?" Thorne asked at once.

"No, sir, but PC Roberts was having a drink at the King's Head just outside Woodstock last night and—er—something came up about the parking there. It was like this. A chap called Alan Hall—he's the manager of the place, and apparently a friend of Roberts—he said they'd had a bit of trouble on Monday evening. A car which sounds as if it might have been Mrs. Thorne's got a dent in the parking lot, and there was a—a fuss."

Abbot stopped, embarrassed. He couldn't repeat all he'd been told. He avoided Thorne's eye, and prayed hard that the Superintendent wouldn't suggest they both go out to Woodstock to investigate.

"What do you mean, a fuss? What sort of place is this King's Head?" Thorne demanded.

"Very respectable, sir. It's really what used to be called a roadhouse. You can have drinks and a meal—the food's good—and dance if you like. There's a cabaret on Saturdays, but not on other nights. It's fairly pricey, but good value."

"You seem to know a lot about it."

"Well—er." Abbot wasn't going to admit to the number of evenings he had spent there with a variety of girlfriends, and Thorne went on without waiting for a comment. "I assume it wouldn't be full on a Monday?"

"No. That's why—" Again Abbot stopped. "There—there really shouldn't have been any trouble in the parking lot, sir. There was plenty of room."

Thorne grunted. "I've asked you once. What sort of trouble? What the hell are you talking about, Sergeant?"

"The couple with the car, sir. Mrs. Thorne—if it was Mrs. Thorne—and the man she was with. If I may make a suggestion, sir, I think you should go and talk to Alan Hall yourself. PC Roberts was really only interested in the car—"

Thorne gave up. It was obvious that his sergeant knew or suspected more than he was prepared to say, and it required an effort not to press him. But admittedly the situation was delicate. "Okay, I will. This evening." To Abbot's relief, Thorne changed the subject. "Found any possibles with a grudge against Sir Leo?" he asked.

"One or two, sir, but I've not finished checking yet."

"Right, Sergeant. Let me know when you have. And let me have the reports on the other characters as soon as possible."

"Yes, sir." Dismissed, Sergeant Abbot gratefully left the office.

The Superintendent's inclination was to abandon Headquarters and visit Woodstock immediately, but he inspected the pile of urgent paperwork on his desk. It was probably a mare's nest, anyway, he reflected. An hour or two would make no difference. Sighing, he picked up his pen in one hand and the microphone of his dictating machine in the other.

Lucy Farling and Stephen Crispin reached Oxford on Wednesday afternoon, Lucy in her new Capri having outdistanced Stephen's ancient Volkswagen by at least fifteen minutes. In Oxford, they had gone their separate ways, Lucy to her College, Crispin to his flat, but had arranged to meet for dinner the next day.

The flat, a converted attic in North Oxford, consisted of two rooms plus a kitchenette and a minute shower room. It was cold and unwelcoming. Crispin lit the gas fire, and went through to the smaller of the rooms. He dropped his bag on his bed, and began to unpack.

He regarded his possessions sourly. The torn jeans could be mended, but they would never look the same again. Nor would the scratched shoes, which had been an expensive luxury. He had been invited to the country for a few days; he had not expected to be forced to climb trees. Nor had he expected to be shot at, and to be a major witness to a murder. His visit to his girlfriend's parents had been full of the unexpected, he thought bitterly.

His possessions put tidily away, he set off for the shops, needing to restore his stock of fresh food after the days he had spent with the Farlings. His telephone was ringing as, burdened with plastic bags, he unlocked the door of his flat. It stopped as he reached it, then started again as he was unpacking in the kitchenette. This time he managed to answer it.

"Hello!" he said, hoping it might be a call from his literary agent, or failing this someone who wanted some private coaching.

"Crispin?" The voice was tough and abrupt.

"Er—yes. I'm Stephen Crispin."

"You've just been staying with Farling?"

"Sir Leo? Yes. But— Who's that? Is it the police?"

The laugh that came over the line was chilling. "No, Crispin, this is not the police. Their opposite numbers, you might say."

For a moment, Crispin was nonplussed. Then, "What do you want?" he asked.

"I want to know what you told the fuzz about what you saw last night, when that bloody Carter got shot."

"Carter?"

"Yes, Carter, damn it. Who else got shot? You were lucky."

"You—you're the man that shot Carter!"

"That's right. But I missed you, Crispin. I don't often miss. I won't a second time."

The threat was direct and Crispin clenched his teeth. The situation was preposterous, and he had no idea how to respond. At last he managed to stammer, "It—it's nothing to do with me."

"Don't be a fool, Crispin. You were there, weren't you? You saw what happened. What did you tell the fuzz? Did you describe the—the one Carter pulled the mask off?"

Stephen Crispin thought fast. If he said yes, they might decide to kill him out of spite, or to prevent him becoming a witness. If he said no, they might kill him to ensure his continuing silence. They'd had no trouble tracing him, it seemed, and he saw no reason to doubt their menace. The best course was to admit a little, but nothing that mattered.

"I told the fuzz—the police—that I thought it was a woman from her figure, but I couldn't describe her face. I'm a bit short-sighted." It was a mixture of fact and fiction. There was nothing wrong with his eyesight, but he didn't believe they could know this.

"Okay." It was a reluctant acceptance, but an acceptance nevertheless, and Crispin sighed with relief. "But keep it like that," the voice went on. "If you're shown any mug shots, don't raise an eyebrow. Softly, softly. Quiet, quiet. Or else. You understand?"

"Yes—yes. I understand."

"You know what'll happen if you try to play silly buggers?"

"Yes. I said yes. And I won't. I can't."

The man at the other end of the line slammed down his phone as Crispin was speaking, and Crispin put his receiver down slowly. He leant against the wall, his eyes tight shut. He was trembling, he realized, as he tried to remember what he had in fact said to the police.

Bert Parker and Willie Burwash were huddled over the paraffin stove in their garden hut. The number of cigarette butts in the tin lid that served them as an ashtray was indicative of their state of nerves, as were the empty beer cans on the floor. Of the two, Parker's feelings were showing more clearly. Burwash was inclined to laugh and swagger, though in reality he too was far from happy.

"Why the hell did Eddie have to take a shooter?" Parker said.

"We don't know it was him," Burwash protested.

"What difference does it make? You know the Mulls. One for all and all for one, that's their motto." Parker felt the bruise marks on his throat. "Besides, with the law what it is now, you don't have to pull the trigger, you just have to be there. Like us."

"No, not like us. We were never in the house." Burwash laughed again. "I wonder how the old Judge's orchids are doing; maybe they've frozen to death already."

"Sod the orchids! It was a bloody stupid trick anyway. It's Carter I'm worried about. Can't you get it through your thick head, Willie? They could send us down on a murder charge."

"And I'm telling you, Bert, not us." Burwash ticked the points off on his fingers as he spoke. "First, there's no reason to suspect us. Second, they've got no evidence against us. Third, if they did get on to the Mulls, Eddie wouldn't squeal. Why should he?"

"He might think it was us who'd shopped him."

"But we haven't, and we're not going to. We just swear we were home in our beds all night and know bloody nothing."

"Jean heard us go out," Parker objected. "So did the kids. And Jean won't let them lie about it for our sakes."

"Okay, we were out shooting rabbits, then. If the worst comes to the worst we'll admit to having a go at the greenhouses—that's just vandalism. After all, we *are* innocent, my old Bert. It was only chance we chose the same night as the Mulls. No one can pin the robbery—or Carter —on us."

"They can have a bloody good try," Parker said glumly.

The man in charge of the case, the man who would be delighted to have a good try, Superintendent George Thorne, had other things on his mind at that moment. He had found the King's Head without difficulty a little beyond Woodstock and, having parked his car, had gone into the bar.

It was still early and the place was almost empty, though all the dim lighting was on, discreet music came from concealed loudspeakers, and the barman was polishing glasses. Thorne ordered a pint of bitter, took a deep drink, and looked about him. Abbot had described the scene aptly, he thought. It looked expensive, and very pleasant. He could imagine himself bringing Miranda here for some special occasion.

He winced as he recalled that she might well have already visited this very bar, and without him. Then, with a motion of his head, he summoned the barman. "Is Mr. Hall here? I'd like a word with him if it's not inconvenient."

"He's around. What name shall I say?"

"Detective-Superintendent Thorne."

The barman stared. Thorne, with his military bearing and neat moustache, looked more like an army officer than a policeman. Then, "Very good, sir." He turned his back and spoke quickly into an intercom; Thorne couldn't hear what was said.

A minute or two later a man came into the bar. "Superintendent Thorne? I'm Alan Hall. What can I do for you? No trouble, I hope."

Alan Hall was short and stocky. He, too, sported a moustache, but his was of the kind favoured by fighter pilots in World War Two—though in fact he could hardly have been born at the time of the Battle of Britain. He held out his hand, and gripped Thorne's firmly. His voice was deep, rich and assured. The Superintendent assessed him as a competent businessman, who would run his pub with strict efficiency, bending the rules only when he thought it expedient.

"No, no trouble," Thorne said. "I gather you had enough of that on Monday night."

Hall allowed himself to register surprise. "Surely you've not come here about that, Superintendent? Not an officer of your rank. Anyway, it's finished and done with."

"Perhaps it isn't. The car in question may have been stolen."

"Yes, but—"

Thorne glanced at the barman, who was listening with interest. "Is there somewhere we could talk privately?"

"Of course. My office." Hall didn't hesitate. "Bring the Superintendent a whisky chaser, Dave, and my usual, will you?"

Hall led the way to a room off a corridor behind the bar. It was furnished as an office but, like the rest of the establishment, smartly and expensively. Hall waved the Superintendent to a comfortable chair, and himself sat behind the desk. The drinks came at once.

Thorne sipped the large malt appreciatively. "Very

nice," he said. "Thanks." He guessed that Hall's colourless drink with its twist of lemon—a gin and tonic?—was almost entirely non-alcoholic. "Now, Mr. Hall, would you mind telling me exactly what did happen here last Monday evening?"

"Sure. But there's not much to tell."

At some time about six-thirty a couple had come into the bar. The man was tall, dark, about forty and handsome enough to be a film star. The woman was much the same age, medium height, plump, curly brown hair and wearing a bright red dress. They had each had two or three drinks, and then left.

"That was when the trouble started. They came back to the bar, demanded to see the manager, and said that while they'd been drinking, someone must have parked beside them and dented their offside bumper. They insisted I should go and look." Hall sighed. "It was a yellow Mini, this year's model and, sure enough, it had a dent which could have been new. But what was I supposed to do about it?"

"What did you do?" Thorne asked.

"In the end, nothing. I offered to call the police, but they didn't want that. Frankly, I don't know what they did want. But they made one hell of a fuss, blamed the establishment, blamed me, said they'd never come to the King's Head again. I only hope they keep their promise," the manager concluded sourly.

"You don't remember the licence number, I suppose?" Thorne said.

"I'm afraid not. Nor did I get their names." Hall shook his head, "I never thought. The whole thing seemed like such a storm in a teacup. Cars are always getting little prangs in parking lots. Though, come to think of it, ours was pretty empty on Monday." He paused for a moment, obviously working it out. Then he added, "But if the car was pinched as you suggested, Superintendent, it was a pretty mad way to behave, wasn't it? Drawing attention to themselves—and the car—like that."

"Yes." Thorne was forced to agree. He was thinking hard. It could have been Miranda's Mini. And certainly the description fitted her, though the description of the man meant nothing to him. Finally he said, "I gather they spent a fair bit of time in the bar. Were they at all drunk, do you think?"

"No-o. Not over the limit, I'd say. Look, would you like to speak to Dave Gosling, the barman? I'll send him in to the office."

"That would be fine," said the Superintendent. "And thanks very much."

"Sorry I couldn't be more help. Just wait here."

Hall disappeared with a cheery wave of his hand, but it was several minutes before the barman arrived. Thorne wondered if Hall was briefing him, but knew he was being oversuspicious; the manager of the King's Head had been completely cooperative.

So was Dave Gosling. He apologized for the delay; Mr. Hall had had to find someone to take his place. He remembered the couple, quite apart from the business with their car, because it was Monday and he'd had few customers. But he didn't know them, had never seen them before.

Questioned, his description corresponded with those volunteered by Hall. And the barman remembered two further facts: they had spoken of the fun they'd had at St. Giles' Fair that afternoon, and they had addressed each other as John and Miranda.

CHAPTER 10

George Thorne slept little that night. While his body tossed and turned in unavailing attempts to make itself comfortable, his mind worked overtime, leaping from one case to another, from one subject to the next until, as at last he began to doze, his thoughts merged into nightmares from which he kept starting awake, sweating and disoriented. He thought at times of getting up and finding a drink or making himself tea or toast or something, but immediately lassitude overcame him. It was not until towards morning that he fell into a deep, if troubled, sleep.

The telephone woke him. At some point in the night he had turned off his alarm clock, and he saw with disgust that it was now after nine. Assuming it was Headquarters calling, he lifted the receiver and barked, "Superintendent Thorne!"

A slightly startled voice answered. "George. George, it's Mary Band."

"Mary? Yes?" Thorne was terse.

It was not the ideal opening for a conversation to which Mary had not been looking forward, but she persevered. "George, if you're still—still on your own next weekend, will you come and have supper on Saturday? Stay overnight if you like, and spend Sunday with us. It's Dick's weekend off, so—so at least he won't be called out in the middle."

"Middle? Middle of what?" asked Thorne stupidly.

"Of your visit, of course, George."

"Oh, I'm sorry, Mary. I've just woken up. You're awfully kind, but I'm not sure—"

"George, please come—please. It'll just be us, and you don't have to be sociable unless you want to."

Thorne hesitated. By Saturday it would be the best part of a week since Miranda had gone, had disappeared. After last night and what he had learnt at the King's Head, he could no longer use the word "abducted," even to himself. But his resolve to make some personal contact with his wife—even if it turned out to be a final meeting—had not wavered. He must . . . He must . . . Or he would never face himself, or the world, again.

A slight cough from the other end of the line recalled him to reality. Maybe a discussion would help, he thought. Perhaps the Bands might suggest some aspect of the matter he had overlooked; in any case it would be a relief to talk to sympathetic, discreet and unofficial ears.

"All right. Thanks, Mary—very much. I'll be there. Subject, of course, to—"

"I know. I know. Don't forget I'm a doctor's wife. Come about seven in time for a drink or two."

No sooner had Thorne replaced his receiver than the phone rang again. This time it was Blackwell's bookshop. A rather breathless voice asked to speak to Mrs. Thorne.

"My wife is away at present," Thorne said. "What is it you want?"

"Away?" There was surprise in the voice as it hurried on. "Mr. Thorne, Mrs. Thorne was in the shop yesterday afternoon. She bought several books. Expensive reference books, they were, so she decided to charge them on her VISA card. Unfortunately she dropped her card, and didn't notice. I found it on the floor as I was clearing up."

Thorne thought quickly. Miranda usually used the public library; she rarely bought expensive books these days. Most of the reference works she needed for her crosswords and acrostics she already owned. But she hadn't taken them with her. So had she replaced them at Blackwell's yesterday? He couldn't question the girl on the phone; he would have to talk to her. He said, "Thank you for letting me know. I'll be in some time today—

probably this morning—to pick it up. Will you keep it for me?"

"Yes, sir, of course. Thank you. I'll be here all day. My name's Verity Pearson, so ask for me—"

Thorne washed, shaved and dressed quickly. He skipped breakfast and left his bed unmade. On Saturday, he promised himself—unless he had to work—he would clean the house, get in a fresh supply of food and do some washing. His domestic situation was becoming desperate, he reflected: he was running out of clean shirts, apart from anything else.

He drove fast to Kidlington. Since yesterday a lot of work had been done on what was already known as the "Farling case," much of it useless, but some that could prove important. Thorne read the reports on his desk, and sent for Abbot, who arrived with a file under his arm and a tray in his hands.

"I hope you'll forgive the liberty, sir. I know it's early, but I expect we'll be paying some calls this morning and I doubt if we'll get much hospitality."

"Thanks, Sergeant." Gratefully Thorne pulled the tray towards him. "We'll be calling on villains, you think?"

He took the file that Abbot was offering, and sifted quickly through it. Finally he nodded, though it was hard to tell whether this was because he had enjoyed his coffee and biscuits, or because he approved of the papers he had read. Abbot waited patiently.

"Right," Thorne said, pushing back his chair. "Let's go. We'll start with the most likely—those sent down by Sir Leo who came out of prison in the last twelve weeks and are living around here. But first I must go to Blackwell's."

"Blackwell's? Yes, sir." Abbot hid his surprise.

He expected the Superintendent to offer some explanation during the drive into Oxford, but none was forthcoming and, to his annoyance, he was left sitting in the car while Thorne went into the shop. In fact, once inside, Thorne demanded Verity Pearson and was directed to the

Reference Department. He hurried down into the galler-
ied well of the store, walls of books rising about him.

"You're Mr. Thorne?" A pretty girl with long fair hair
regarded him through enormous spectacles. "I'm Verity
Pearson."

Thorne could see she wore no wedding ring, so he said,
"Yes, Miss Pearson. You were kind enough to phone to say
you'd found my wife's VISA card."

"I've got it right here."

"Thank you." Thorne waited while she rummaged in a
drawer of the desk. He wanted more than merely to claim
Miranda's credit card; he wanted information, but it was
difficult to know how to word his questions. "You knew my
wife quite well, I expect?" he ventured at length.

"Oh no, sir. But her name was on the card, and she
mentioned that she lived locally so I looked her up in the
phone book."

"I see. Clever of you. You're sure it was she who actually
used the card?"

"Yes. Why, yes." Miss Pearson frowned. "There's no
trouble, is there? We did the usual phone check on the
card itself, and the signatures tallied. She was—well, she
was quite a plump lady—dark, fortyish, wearing a yellow
suit. She—she hadn't stolen the card, had she? And
shouldn't I ask for some identification before giving it to
you?"

"Of course," Thorne said quickly, thinking that unfortunately the girl was intelligent. "Would my own VISA card
do?" He produced it, knowing that it made no reference
to his rank. "No trouble about the books, but I'm afraid my
wife was taken ill last night, and it's important to know if
she was behaving normally earlier yesterday."

"I—I see. You said she'd gone away." It was almost an
accusation.

"To a nursing home," Thorne improvised.

"Oh dear!" Miss Pearson thought for a moment. "Well,
she seemed fine when she was here. She had a list, and she

knew exactly what she wanted. But you should ask the gentleman she was with."

This time Thorne was not surprised. "Tall, dark, good-looking?"

"Well, tall and dark, yes. I know they were together, because I had to go upstairs and I saw him take the bag of books from her as they left the shop."

Thorne nodded, implying that he could identify his wife's companion; certainly by now he was beginning to recognize the description. "Thank you very much, Miss Pearson. You've been a great help." He made to turn away, then swung back. "I suppose you couldn't remember the books my wife bought?"

"She didn't take them home?" Verity Pearson asked at once.

"No—no. She must have mislaid them later." Thorne knew it was a weak excuse, and smiled apologetically.

Miss Pearson hesitated. Then, "Yes, I think I can. They were all related. I'll try to jot down the titles for you. Or our stock department could help."

"No, please—"

A glance at the list as he was going up the stairs brought Thorne a moment of genuine satisfaction. There were five titles, all ones that Miranda had left behind at home, but that she would need to help compile her puzzles. If nothing else, this meant that she hadn't abandoned her hobby. She would be sending in her crosswords and acrostics as usual. She would be in touch with Ian Dawson, the editor of the very reputable literary magazine, published in London, to which she was a regular and valued contributor. Through Dawson, he should himself be able to contact her.

He was grinning broadly, if absently, when he came out of Blackwell's. Abbot opened the car door for him, and regarded him inquiringly. But Thorne gave no explanation.

"Where to now, sir?" Abbot asked.

"As we're in Oxford, we'll try Hudson," Thorne said. "I remember him threatening Sir Leo from the dock when he was sentenced."

The former convict, however, was in bed with a high temperature. A doctor was leaving the house as the police officers arrived, and there was no doubt that the illness was genuine. It was inconceivable that Hudson could have been out and about the previous night, taking part in an armed robbery.

"Okay. Colombury next. We'll try Parker and Burwash," Thorne said without being asked. "Let's hope for better luck there."

Jean Haule was not in the best of tempers. She had a very heavy cold which was keeping her away from her work, and she was worried. She was worried about the shop of which she was the manageress, where she should have been this Thursday morning. She was worried about her son, who wasn't doing well at school. And she was worried about Bert and Willie; she was certain they had been up to something.

She had heard them leave the house on Tuesday night, and had dozed restlessly until their return. The next morning at breakfast Bert had been subdued, while Willie was excessively exuberant. She had recognized the signs, but with the kids around it had been impossible to ask questions, and as soon as the kids went to school, the two men retreated to their wretched shed. Since then, she had felt too unwell to confront them.

Now the doorbell rang, and she went to answer it. She knew immediately that the two men were police. She had no need for Thorne's formal statement, or the warrant card that he produced.

"Yes, I'm Mrs. Haule. What do you want?"

"A few words with your brother, Bert Parker, and with Willie Burwash. I believe they're both living here."

"They're not here now."

Jean made to shut the door, but Abbot's shoe was too quick for her. For a moment the scene remained static, as the two detectives waited in silence.

"I told you. They're not here," Jean repeated.

"Then perhaps you'll answer some questions for us yourself, Mrs. Haule."

"What about?"

"Let's talk inside, shall we? I'm sure your neighbours are as curious as most."

Reluctantly Jean opened the door. "You've got no right, hounding people like this," she said indignantly. "Bert and Willie have paid for what they did. How can you expect them to live decent lives if you're always on the doorstep, accusing them of things they've never done? What is it this time?"

"We'd just like a little help with some inquiries," Thorne said mildly.

Jean Haule showed them into the front room. From there they couldn't see the garden, but any moment Bert or Willie might decide to come back to the house, to use the loo, to cadge some cigarettes, to make a cup of tea. She didn't ask the detectives to sit down.

"So what do you want to know?" she demanded truculently.

"Are you sure your brother and his friend aren't available? They're both still on parole, you know," Thorne said, giving a small smile.

It was no more than a ploy on the Superintendent's part but it had its effect. Jean, already apprehensive, assumed he knew more than he did. Even before she spoke she knew her expression had given her away.

"Maybe they're in the garden," she admitted. "I'll go and see, shall I?"

"Yes, please do, Mrs. Haule," Thorne agreed. "Sergeant Abbot will go with you."

Jean glared at the Superintendent, but didn't argue and Abbot, hiding his grin, followed her through the kitchen and into the so-called garden. In reality, this consisted of a patch of weedy grass, a few tired shrubs, a neglected vegetable patch—and a shed. There was no one in sight, and Abbot's first reaction was that Thorne had been mistaken.

But Jean called out loudly, "Bert! Willie! You've got visitors. Important visitors!"

The door of the shed opened almost at once. Parker and Burwash emerged, carefully shutting the door behind them. Abbot caught only a glimpse of playing cards on a table, and a couple of chairs.

"Fuzz," Jean said briefly and unnecessarily. "Sergeant Abbot. Superintendent Thorne's in the front room."

"Bloody hell!" Bert said. "So what are we meant to have done now?" He spat deliberately, hiding his nervousness.

When Abbot didn't answer, Parker pushed past the Sergeant into the house. Abbot made the mistake of following him. The movements gave Burwash, who so far had shown no emotion, a chance to catch hold of Jean's arm and whisper, "We never went out on Tuesday night. Understand?"

She nodded dumbly, thinking, Oh God! I was right: they *have* been up to something.

In the front room Superintendent Thorne had made himself comfortable in an armchair, his back to the window. He waved to the rest of them to find seats. "You've heard about the robbery at Sir Leo Farling's house early yesterday morning," he began chattily.

"No!" Jean said involuntarily.

Thorne glanced at her, eyebrows raised. "Don't you take a newspaper, or ever listen to the radio or watch television, Mrs. Haule?"

"Not yesterday. I came home from work early because I had a bad cold and I went to bed and—and I haven't seen this morning's paper yet."

"What about you?" Thorne turned to the two men, sprawled on the sofa.

"We did see a bit in the paper," Burwash said. "But no reason why we should be interested, is there?"

"Armed robbery," Thorne mused. "Used to be your line once, didn't it? Of course you never killed anyone. Too bad about the Farlings' houseman, wasn't it? Killing in commission of a crime. It'll be a murder charge, you know, for all those involved, not just for the chap who used his shooter."

"Here, wait a minute," said Burwash. "What's all this? You can't pin that job on us, you can't. So don't try. We were here all night Tuesday, Bert and me. We never left the house. Jean'll vouch for it. Won't you, Jean?"

There was only the slightest hesitation before Jean Haule said firmly, "Sure, they were here. I'd have heard them if they'd gone out. This place is made of cardboard."

Thorne seemingly accepted the alibis, though he knew they were worthless, and continued with his questions. Abbot noticed that for no clear reason, the Superintendent took special care to name and describe the members of the Farling household. Apparently he learnt little but, getting up to leave, he thanked them all politely for being so helpful; he knew from experience that such gratitude often worried people with things to hide. They regarded him warily, but didn't respond.

Going down the short path, the front door shut behind them, Abbot said, "Don't you wish you were a fly, sir, so you could hear what they're saying now? Or that we were able to use bugs?"

Thorne nodded grimly. "But still, it wasn't unsatisfactory," he said. "Personally, I think the woman's in the clear. Apart from lying, I mean. She was protecting her men, but I'd swear the robbery and the killing were news to her."

"But you think the men know something about it?"

The Superintendent got into their car. "More than they told us, that's for sure. Willie Burwash definitely blenched when I mentioned Joyce Greene's name. Of course there's no reason why he shouldn't know the Farlings' pretty maid, and his mate showed no reaction, but—" He shook his head.

There was a pause until Abbot said, "Did you notice their feet, sir?"

"Not particularly. Why?"

"Burwash's are normal, small if anything, but Parker's are large. The right one might fit snugly into that print we found in the Judge's garden."

"M—mm. That's a point," Thorne said thoughtfully. "Burwash and Parker to riddle the glasshouses. But who else to commit the robbery? I refuse to believe Jean Haule was the woman that chap Crispin says he saw."

Abbot, ready to drive off, waited expectantly, but Thorne remained silent and eventually the Sergeant was forced to ask his standard question. "Where to now, sir?"

"Oh, let's try the local police station again. Maybe Sergeant Court is back. For courtesy's sake we need a word with him as we're on his patch."

Thorne said no more till they were in the centre of Colombury, and Abbot made no effort to interrupt his superior's thoughts. Then the Superintendent said suddenly, "There were too many villains in this affair at the Farlings', and that's why we'll catch them. When you turn to crime, Sergeant, keep those involved to a minimum."

CHAPTER 11

Superintendent Thorne and Sergeant Abbot spent more time in the Colombury police station than Thorne had intended. His opinion of Sergeant Court was not high; he considered him well-meaning, but slow and inept—a typical country police officer. His greatest virtue was that he seemed to be aware of his own shortcomings, and had no hesitation in appealing to Headquarters for assistance. But Court had another virtue which Thorne had momentarily forgotten: his long years of experience in the one area had given him an unsurpassed knowledge of the inhabitants of Colombury and its surrounding villages. In fact, Sergeant Court could be said to represent "community policing" of the most effective order.

"Joyce Greene?" he answered slowly. "Yes, of course I know her, sir—a pretty girl, but a worry to her mother. Mrs. Greene's a widow. Her husband died of leukaemia when Joyce was a baby, and Vera Greene's had a tough time since."

"And why's Joyce a worry to her ma?" asked Thorne.

"She's flirty." Court hesitated, glancing quickly at Abbot, who had failed to hide his amusement at his fellow sergeant's archaic choice of adjective. "Always after young men, and going to these discos. It's surprising to me she's not got into trouble before this."

"We don't know she's in trouble now," Thorne commented shortly. "Let's not jump to conclusions. And what about Grace Davis? I expect you know her, too?"

"Yes, sir. She's a different type of girl altogether. Steady, reliable. In fact, she's a cousin of mine by marriage."

"Is she, indeed?" Thorne remembered that he had once remarked that Sergeant Court seemed to be related to every individual in the Colombury area, but the officer's myriad connections still surprised him. "And what do you know about Mrs. Haule—Jean Haule?"

"The one from the council houses?" Court asked, while Thorne waited, silently cursing the ponderous consideration the local sergeant seemed to give to every simple query.

"She's the manageress of that clothes shop in the High Street," Abbot intervened as he saw that his superintendent's patience was about to snap. "And she's Bert Parker's sister."

Court nodded. "Yes, for her sins, poor woman—"

"Would the Greene girl and Grace Davis know her?"
Thorne interrupted.

"From the shop, perhaps," said Court, "but I'd think not
otherwise. She keeps herself to herself, does Jean Haule."

"Might either of the girls know Bert Parker himself—or
Willie Burwash?" Thorne inquired, doing his best to contain his temper.

"Young Grace wouldn't, that's for sure." For once Sergeant Court reacted quickly, and indignantly. "She
wouldn't mix with known villains. But that Joyce Greene,
now, I wouldn't like to speak for her."

Court lapsed into thoughtful silence, his brows fur-
rowed in a frown. Thorne waited expectantly, hoping,
Abbot thought, for the next pearl of wisdom. None came
immediately, however, and Thorne looked at his watch,
then cleared his throat, making as if to depart.

"Sir," Court said finally. "Maybe I shouldn't ask, but are
you suggesting that Joyce Greene gave Parker and Burwash information that helped them to get into Sir Leo's
house?"

"The point had crossed my mind, Sergeant, yes." The
Superintendent didn't attempt to hide his sarcasm.

However, Court appeared not to notice. He was shaking his head vigorously. "If you'll forgive me for saying so,
sir, I'm sure you're wrong. Parker and Burwash are bad
hats right enough, but they'd not have shot a man in cold
blood."

"Maybe their blood wasn't so cold," Thorne said. "After
all, they went to jail for armed robbery."

"In my opinion, that verdict wasn't absolutely fair, sir—
not the armed part." Court spoke with surprising empha-
sis. "Look, sir. Burwash just had a cosh, but you know as
well as I do that all the wise guys carry them nowadays; it's
supposed to make them feel 'macho,' if that's the word."
Court paused, apparently surprised at his own lengthy
speech. Then he went on, "Parker—now he had one of
those Swiss knives—the ones with all those blades and

attachments, even a pair of scissors sometimes—quite a small thing. But they didn't use either of the weapons, if they were really intended as weapons. Parker said he didn't even realize he was carrying the knife, because it was always in his pocket. It's all a long way from shooting, I'd say, sir."

Thorne had the grace to acknowledge that this was so, and Court smiled with satisfaction. It was lucky, Abbot thought, that Court didn't hear Thorne's comment as they set off for the Farlings' house.

"I wonder," the Superintendent said morosely, "I wonder if that Sergeant Court is related, by marriage or in any other way, to Parker or Burwash."

Parker and Burwash had again retreated to their garden shed. The row with Jean after the police had gone had been brief, but fierce. Jean had threatened Bert and Willie with eviction from her house unless she heard the full story, and immediately. At first reluctantly, and then with surprising eagerness, they had complied.

"And you swear that's the truth?" she demanded. "You didn't go into the Farlings' house? You had no part in the burglary? Or the shooting? You know nothing whatsoever about them? It was pure chance you happened to be around, peppering the old Judge's orchids?"

Both men swore they were innocent of anything except an attempt to work off a grudge, and the fact that they seemed glad to tell their side of the story carried some conviction. Jean reached the conclusion that they were indeed telling the truth—probably almost the whole truth.

She herself had of course already lied on their behalf, but her action had been instinctive. It was only slowly that she had begun to realize the full enormity of the situation in which they—and now she—were inescapably involved. Murder. Deliberate murder, in the course of robbery.

They could go down for years; she herself could go to prison. And what would happen to the children then?

At the thought, her nerve snapped. "Get out!" she screamed at them. "Get out of the house! Go and play in your filthy little shed. Get drunk if you want to! I wish—I wish—"

Bursting into tears, Jean Haule had run upstairs, and the two men had, rather sheepishly, made their way into the garden. Now they faced each other across the card table. Parker was pale, the freckles on his skin standing out like liver marks. Burwash, on the other hand, was flushed. Oddly enough Jean's outburst had shaken them more than Thorne's interrogation.

"Will she shop us?" Burwash asked.

"My sister? No. Never." Parker was positive. "She'll calm down. But we mustn't let her know about Eddie." Tentatively he touched his neck; the bruises hidden by the polo-neck of his sweater still hurt. "Her—or anybody. For our own sakes, as well as Eddie's. If the fuzz do get on to him somehow, we don't want any connection between us."

"No," said Burwash, and wondered if he should warn Parker that a connection wouldn't be hard to establish. He decided to try another tack first. "The shotgun Eddie gave us—" he began.

"We'll give it back. We don't need it any more."

"Okay, but—Bert, there's something you'd better know. I did Eddie a kind of favour the other day."

Parker stared at Burwash. "What sort of favour?"

"That girl the Superintendent was on about. Joyce Greene. Eddie asked me to pick her up at a disco, chat her up a bit—you know—and find out what I could about the set-up at the Judge's place."

"And now you tell me! You bloody fool!" Parker swore violently. "She'll remember all right. You've put us straight in the shit, you have," he said angrily. "Can't you see further than the end of that blasted nose of yours?"

It was only an hour later before they realized just how deep in the shit they were. Superintendent Thorne had been on the radio to Headquarters, and a Thames Valley police van with four uniformed officers drew up in the road outside Jean Haule's house.

Jean Haule greeted the party at the front door. They had no search warrant, but after some expostulation, Jean waived the need for one, knowing perfectly well that the document could be produced in a matter of hours. She watched as the officers quickly discovered the shotgun in the garden shed and removed it, together with various bits of Bert's and Willie's clothing, including some of their shoes.

They also removed Bert and Willie, inviting them to come to Kidlington "to assist with certain inquiries." Bert and Willie protested vigorously, but in the end had no option. The officers did not ask Jean to come too, and her children, returning from school, found her sitting on the stairs, gazing into space.

"Little Joyce Greene!" Sir Leo Farling shook his head sadly. "I wouldn't have thought it of her. In my experience, it's usually the plain girls without any boyfriends who get led astray. Don't you agree, Superintendent?"

"Yes, sir," said Thorne, wondering idly how Sergeant Court would have reacted to this homespun generalization.

"What will happen to her?" Helen Farling asked.

"Nothing much," said Sir Leo. "First offence. Probation, I imagine. So don't worry about her, my dear." He turned to Thorne. "You've been very efficient, Superintendent."

"Thank you, sir. But the case isn't solved yet. We still don't know who shot your houseman. I think we'll be able to prove that Burwash and Parker were in the grounds on Wednesday morning, that they did wanton damage to your glasshouse, and thus to some of your orchids, and that there's some connection between them and the robbery. But I wouldn't like to go further than that at the moment, sir."

"I remember Parker and Burwash—an odd pair and not too bright," Sir Leo said reminiscently. "Parker lost his temper when I sentenced him, and swore he'd get his own back. Not that I paid any attention. As far as I've been able to tell it's the quiet ones—the broody ones—who are most likely to seek some kind of revenge, not the ones who let fly."

"What I can't understand is why two of the gang did their best to wake us up by pouring buckshot into our greenhouses, while the other two were trying to be as quiet as possible inside the house," Lady Farling said. "The whole thing seems silly."

"Many villains are stupid, Helen," Sir Leo said, somewhat pompously. "That's the only reason they get caught."

Thorne, while he agreed with the first part of the Judge's comment, felt that the second half was scarcely complimentary to his own profession. No great respecter of persons, he said curtly, "In which case we must hope that the pair who actually burglarized your house are among the stupid, Sir Leo. Otherwise you and Lady Farling may not get your possessions back."

"But surely Parker and Burwash will give their accomplices away," Helen Farling protested. "Why should they protect them?"

The Superintendent took a deep breath, and Abbot prayed that Thorne wasn't going to make some acid remark he might later regret. The Sergeant need not have worried. Thorne merely gave a not very convincing smile, and said, "I hope to be in a better position to tell you that, Lady Farling, when I've questioned these men. So—if you'll excuse us?"

Lady Farling's question was one that Abbot himself would have liked answered and, driving back to

Kidlington, he couldn't resist the temptation. "Do you
think they'll cough, sir?" he asked.

This time Thorne gave a direct answer. "It'll all depend
on whether they're more scared of us and what we can do
to them than they are of what the other villains can manage. But at least this morning's efforts have convinced me
of something, Sergeant: Parker and Burwash aren't our
main objectives."

About to swing into a space in the parking lot beside
Thames Valley Police Headquarters, Sergeant Abbot
braked violently. Even then he only missed the old Volkswagen Beetle by half an inch. He gulped. "Sorry, sir!"

But Thorne was already leaping out of his car. The
Volkswagen had stopped, too, and the Superintendent
was tapping on its window to make the driver lower it.
Stephen Crispin obeyed slowly. It was clear that Thorne
was the last officer he wanted to encounter.

"Hello, Mr. Crispin," Thorne greeted him with an obviously false bonhomie. "What are you doing here? Helping
the police with their inquiries, eh?"

Crispin did not consider the quip amusing. "You could
say that," he replied stolidly, "though I wasn't much
help."

"You didn't recognize the woman intruder you saw at
the Farlings, not from all those mug shots you've been
shown?" Thorne no longer made a pretence of ignorance
of the reason for Crispin's visit to Headquarters.

"No!" In fact, Crispin was lying, for he could have identified the pale face with the pointed features and the short
reddish hair that he had seen grappling with Carter in the
hall of the Manor in the small hours of Wednesday morning. But he remembered that dreadful voice on the
phone.

"Ah, I thought perhaps you mightn't."

With this possibly ambiguous comment, Thorne
sketched a salute and hurried into the building, leaving

Crispin gently sweating. Abbot grinned at him, parked his own car, and ran after the Superintendent. He caught up with Thorne by the lift.

"Maybe we've got something," Thorne said.

But their hopes proved fruitless. Crispin had been extremely nervous the whole time he had been looking at the mug shots, but he had shown no reaction to any particular face. Nor, except for a dangerous driving charge that had been dropped for lack of evidence, did he show up on records. Shrugging off his disappointment, Thorne sent for Bert Parker; at least they'd got something on him.

"Sit down," Thorne said abruptly, pointing to the chair on the other side of his desk.

Parker sat, put his hands in his pockets, and crossed his legs. His intention was to appear nonchalant, but in reality he only succeeded in looking wary. Thorne nodded at Abbot. Without speaking, Abbot spread a piece of newspaper on the desk, and carefully planted a large shoe in the middle of it.

Parker stared at it. "That's—that's mine," he said after a long silence.

"Right," Thorne agreed.

"What's it doing here?"

"Evidence."

"What of? You've got nothing against me."

"Haven't we?" Suddenly Thorne leaned across the desk, and spoke crisply. "Then perhaps you'd explain how your shoe exactly fits a print mark left in Sir Leo Farling's garden early last Wednesday morning. Soil taken from it hasn't yet been analysed, but I've no doubt it will match. You also caught a thread from your sweater on a shrub. Need I say more—except that you're already just out on parole?"

There was another pause while Parker took this in. Then, "You going to charge me?" he said.

"Yes." Thorne gave the formal caution. "Malicious dam-

age will do for now. There will probably be other charges
to follow."

"Such as?"

"Accessory to murder. And in the circumstances that
could mean a long stretch. With your record you'll be an
old man by the time you come out."

Parker's tongue tried to moisten his dry lips. "You can't
pin no murder charge on me," he said, grammar forgotten in his distress. "I know nothing about no murder." He
swallowed hard. "Okay. I'll admit to being there at the old
Judge's—but only outside the house. It was just bad
luck—"

Thorne stopped him. "You mean you want to make a
statement?"

Resignedly Bert Parker nodded; he knew when he was
beaten. He admitted that he and Willie Burwash had
taken a pot-shot at the Judge's greenhouses. He admitted
damaging Lady Farling's car. He denied poisoning Jason,
the Dobermann, and he denied all knowledge of the burglary and the subsequent murder. He was vehement
about that.

Thorne hammered him with questions. Where had he
got the shotgun? Had he been at St. Giles' Fair on Monday
last? Why had Burwash questioned Joyce Greene about
the Farling household? What did he know of Stephen
Crispin?

Parker did his best to appear cooperative, without be-
traying information he thought to be vital. But many of
the Superintendent's questions he failed to understand,
and this scared him. He was baffled at the inquiry about
St. Giles' Fair; sure, he had been there, but not on the
Monday; he had waited till the following day. He knew
nothing of Crispin. He had never met Joyce Greene. The
shotgun belonged to Willie Burwash. He had neither seen
nor heard anyone near the Farlings' house on the night of
the burglary and the subsequent murder. He was shaking
when Thorne had finished with him.

"He knows a lot more," Thorne said when Parker had been led away to the charge room. "Yet even with a murder hanging over him he's scared to tell. I wonder why. Let's see if Willie Burwash is any tougher."

Burwash, who had intentionally been allowed a glimpse of the departing Parker, was in an unhappy position. His story mustn't contradict his mate's. Yet exactly what had his mate told the fuzz? As a result of this classic prisoner's dilemma he had no alternative but to answer in monosyllables whenever he could. Thorne persevered, but in the end he got little except an admission that Burwash had indeed spoken with Joyce Greene about the Farlings, and a statement that the shotgun had been bought from a stranger in a pub. Burwash was as adamant as Parker that he knew nothing of the burglary and the killing.

Thorne smiled sourly as he recalled the Judge's contempt for the two criminals, and Lady Farling's happy optimism that under pressure they would confess all. A lot more hard, slogging police work must take place, he thought, before Robert Carter's murderer was charted. Wistfully, he wished he could have discussed the whole affair with Miranda, as he had discussed so many of his cases in the past.

CHAPTER 12

It was Saturday, and officially Superintendent Thorne was not on duty. On any other rest day he might have slept late, and even been brought his breakfast in bed. Today, however, was different, and he had set his alarm early.

He slipped on some old clothes without bothering to wash or shave, drank a quick mug of coffee and set to work on the house. He stripped the bed and remade it with fresh linen. He collected all the dirty clothes he could find and flung them into the washing-machine. He dusted, vacuumed, swept, cleaned pots and pans. By noon, the place looked reasonably respectable again.

Exhausted, Thorne went into the kitchen and got himself a can of beer from the refrigerator. He sat down at the kitchen table and drank it quickly. He was proud of his domestic efforts, and in a curious way the unaccustomed chores had made him feel closer to Miranda. As he started on a second can, he thought longingly of her. He wondered where she was and what she was doing, and he pictured her, surrounded by the books she had bought at Blackwell's, struggling to compose some word puzzle.

This thought reminded him that he had so far been unable to contact Ian Dawson. When he had phoned before he had been told that the magazine editor was having a short holiday in Paris, and was not expected back in his London office till Monday. Thorne had declined to speak to anyone else, saying it was a private matter. The delay irritated him, but there was nothing he could do about it. He could only hope that when he did manage to speak to him, Dawson, whom he had met only a few times, would be cooperative and prepared to help without asking too many questions.

The phone interrupted him with a message from Headquarters. Mrs. Thorne's car had been found. An observant police constable had spotted it on a used-car lot in Cowley, a "For Sale" notice on its windscreen. Apparently, there had been no attempt to change its appearance, or its licence plate. The business was run by a chap called Bernard Printer, and he had seemingly bought the little yellow Mini a couple of days ago in good faith; he had all the papers necessary to confirm the transaction.

It was with a sense of inevitability that Thorne heard the stolid voice at the other end of the line continue with the report, "The lady who sold the car, sir—she answers to Mrs. Thorne's description and she gave her name and your address." It paused, then went on, "Nevertheless, we've impounded the car on the grounds that it may be stolen property, and we'll give it a good going-over."

"Fine," said Thorne. "Thanks. Anything known against Printer?"

"No, sir. He's got a local reputation as an honest dealer, and he showed us his cheque stub. He paid a reasonable price for the vehicle. Incidentally, we didn't mention your name, but he volunteered that he'd be at his lot all day. So if you'd like to talk to him yourself, sir—"

"I'll do that."

Thorne took down the address, repeated his thanks, and hung up. Though he had avoided showing any signs of it during his conversation, he was totally confused. Why in God's name had Miranda sold her beloved Mini? Was she short of money since she had lost her VISA card? She'd got a cheque-book, and there should be an adequate amount in their joint account. But perhaps she'd already drawn it out? Something else to check up on, he told himself. And, more reluctantly, he asked himself about the man she seemed to be with. Had he no money? Or was it quite simply that they had no more use for two cars?

He told himself that there was nothing to be gained by haste. He needed to eat before he went out. He had a sudden picture of the Chief Constable's face, if one of his senior superintendents were to be charged with drunk driving after two beers on an empty stomach and, in spite of his worries and preoccupations, he grinned. But, as he made an early lunch of bread and jam and a can of peaches, washed down with a mug of tea, he knew he couldn't continue to live with this uncertainty much longer.

Half an hour later he set off for Cowley. Bernard Printer was anxious to cooperate. He was short and squat, with a deformed arm, but no fool, and the last thing he wanted was trouble with the police. Thorne introduced himself as Superintendent George James, omitting his last name.

As Printer told Thorne, he had no reason to doubt this

particular sale. "She was a nice lady," he said, "well spoken and, believe me, I get to know them. I've had all sorts, buyers and sellers. For the life of me, I couldn't see her as a thief. I was so sure I didn't even bother with the list." He meant the list of stolen cars that the police circulated regularly to dealers and garages.

"It wasn't on it," said Thorne, "so don't worry. Did she give any reason why she wanted to part with a comparatively new car?"

"More or less. She said her husband had lost his job, been made redundant, and they were going to need the money. They certainly couldn't afford two cars. She was embarrassed, almost apologetic about it."

"Was her—her husband with her?"

"No. But I guess it was him waiting along the street for her. I saw her get into a blue Metro. I remember wondering vaguely why he'd left the sale to her—maybe he imagined a lady would get a better deal—but it was too far away for me to take the number of the other car, even if I'd thought of it. And that's about all I can tell you."

Thorne nodded. It was true there were hundreds of blue Metros in and around Oxford, but it was almost inconceivable that this one was not the same as the car parked in his own street last Monday morning. The evidence was becoming overwhelming that Miranda was acting of her own free will, and not under duress. He nodded again, gloomily.

"Thanks," he said finally. "I suppose the other officers made a note of your bank and cheque number and so on?"

"Yes," said Printer, eyeing the Superintendent a little doubtfully. There was something out of the ordinary about this yellow Mini, he thought. The police were behaving very oddly. Why a superintendent, in the first place? But it wasn't up to him to question them. However . . . "There is one thing," he said somewhat tentatively. "I paid good money for that car; I bet my cheque's been cashed by now. Have I any hope of seeing it again—the car or the money?"

Printer had expected a non-committal reply, but to his surprise the Superintendent didn't hesitate. "Yes," he said promptly. "I'll make sure you do. You may have to wait a bit. But you'll get your money or the car back. You won't be out of pocket in the end, I promise you."

He left Bernard Printer scratching his head and staring after him, but he didn't care. It was his wife who had sold her car—as she had a perfect right to do—and, even if the circumstances were unusual, he was prepared to take full responsibility, and make sure that no one suffered from her actions. But he was equally determined to trace the reasons for these actions.

That evening, after a couple of whiskies and the first home-cooked meal he'd had for a week, the relaxed atmosphere of the Bands' home had begun to work wonders for George Thorne. Now he felt a need to talk—to articulate aloud his hopes, his doubts, his fears—and he could not have had a more sympathetic audience than Dick and Mary Band. Normally an introverted man, Thorne poured his heart out to them.

"—an awful thing to admit," he said at last, "but I would have faced it more easily—or I think I would—if Miranda had been kidnapped and some demand made on me. But that she should just walk out— It's as if she didn't care a damn about me, and never has. It makes a mockery of our whole marriage."

Dick Band stroked his balding head. "You're quite convinced she went voluntarily?" he said.

"Dear God, I'd like to think she didn't!" said Thorne explosively. "But she was seen leaving the house with her bags, and alone. Then I probably saw her myself at St. Giles' Fair. She was certainly in that Woodstock pub and buying books at Blackwell's, and now she's sold her car—alone again. At any of these times she could have cried for help if she'd wanted to, couldn't she? What can one think? Against all this, there's only the fact that she left her most precious jewellery behind, and didn't bother to phone that Meals on Wheels woman—and—and—finally there's just the point that none of it's *like* Miranda."

"No, it's not like her, not a bit, George," Mary Band agreed at once. "Apart from anything else, she was—is—the most considerate of people."

"I've wondered if she could be ill—amnesia, something like that?" Thorne looked hopefully at the doctor. "Or, to be more far-fetched, if she could be drugged or hypnotized in some way? When she spoke to me on the phone, saying she was never returning, she did sound—not quite herself." He paused, then answered his own questions as Dick Band shook his head. "I know, I know. She's behaved perfectly normally wherever she's been seen. I'm clutching at stupid straws."

He sighed heavily. It was no use; he had to accept that Miranda had left voluntarily. But why? Why? He was unaware that he had spoken aloud until Mary tried to find an answer.

"Is it possible that some threat was made to her?" she asked tentatively. "A kind of blackmail? That if she didn't leave you and do as she was told something dreadful would happen—to you yourself, say."

"I've thought of that," Thorne said doubtfully, "but there's nothing to suggest it—and why?" Fear, he knew, could exert great pressure on individuals, and unexpectedly he thought of Bert Parker and Willie Burwash stewing in their cells. "But I do know this," he added. "I've got to find her and talk to her. I'll never be satisfied till I do!"

"Surely your—your colleagues will help," Mary said.

"They've found the Mini, and they're doing what they can with it." Thorne shrugged. "But the general opinion is that Miranda's walked out on me, and who can blame her. It's an opinion my Chief Constable seems to share," he said bitterly. "At any rate he refuses to consider Miranda a missing person. He says it would be absurd on present evidence, and we're far too short-staffed to go chasing after hares."

"You'll find her, George." Band was reassuring. "It's not as if she's disappeared into thin air. You know she's still in the neighbourhood. She's not tried to hide that fact. On the contrary—"

Indeed, as he said later to his wife while they were going to bed, it was one of the curiosities of the situation that Miranda and the strange man she was with seemed to take every opportunity almost to flaunt their presence.

While the Bands were entertaining George Thorne, Lucy Farling was being entertained by Stephen Crispin. The moment Lucy met him in the bar of the Randolph Hotel in Oxford, she realized it was an occasion. He was wearing a new suit, shirt and tie.

"My, you look smart!" Lucy mocked.

Crispin grinned. "It's a special occasion."

"Is it now?" She was still mocking, but she looked at Stephen sharply. She was accustomed to his moods by now, his ups and his downs, but as a rule they were reasonably predictable and depended almost entirely on the progress of his writing. But tonight he seemed both particularly elated and a little nervous.

Crispin had prepared his approach carefully, but this was not the right time for it. "What'll you have to drink, love?"

"Usual, please."

After drinks they went into the pleasantly full restaurant. For once Crispin had managed to get one of the best tables, in a corner where they could sit side by side on a banquette. They discussed the menu and ordered wine. While they waited for the food they had another drink, and Crispin thought that perhaps the moment was ripe.

"Lucy," he said, and took her hand.

"Yes?" She was surprised. Stephen was not usually given to sentimental gestures in public.

"Did you mean it the other night when you said you'd marry me?"

"Of course I did."

Lucy turned to him, smiling. From his pocket Crispin took a small velvet jeweller's box, and put it on the table. "For you. I'm afraid it's not new. Money wouldn't run to a new one. This was my mother's. I hope you'll like it."

The words came out in a rush, and Crispin waited anxiously as Lucy opened the box and took out the ring. It really was most attractive, diamonds and sapphires in an old-fashioned setting. But if Lucy didn't like it . . .

"It's beautiful—fantastic! Thank you, darling," Lucy said at once, her face bright with pleasure. "And it's extra nice it was your mother's."

Relieved, Crispin sighed. "I hope it fits," he said. "Let me put it on for you."

The ring fitted perfectly and the rest of the evening passed in a haze of happiness. It was not until they were having coffee that anything marred it.

Lucy said, "By the way, I was talking to Dad on the phone last night, and he told me the police have caught two of the gang."

"What? How?" Crispin's hand shook as he put down his cup, spilling coffee on the tablecloth.

Lucy appeared not to notice. "Some guys called Burwash and Parker, a couple of fairly small-time criminals."

"Burwash and Parker," Crispin said stupidly. "Two men? Not the—the—"

"Not the two who killed poor Carter. The two who attacked the orchid house. But with any luck they'll snitch on their chums. There's not much 'honour among thieves' in real life, at least not according to Dad."

Crispin nodded. He couldn't bring himself to speak. He was remembering too vividly that threatening voice on the phone. Nothing, he told himself, nothing would make him identify the woman he had seen lying in the Farlings' hall that night, but if someone else—this Burwash or Parker—did so, then he might, probably would be, blamed, and . . . With difficulty he repressed a shudder. Lucy failed to understand why the rest of the evening, in and out of bed, was a disaster.

CHAPTER 13

The Thames Valley Police Force had not been idle over the weekend. When Superintendent Thorne came into his office on Monday morning a stack of files awaited him, together with Sergeant Abbot. The Sergeant was looking tired—his current girlfriend was very demanding—but quite pleased with life.

"Good morning, sir," Abbot greeted his superior.

"Tell me one good thing about it," replied Thorne, staring gloomily at his desk.

Abbot grinned cheerfully. "A possible lead on the Farling case, sir, and a report on Mrs. Thorne's car—there, on top."

Thorne quickly leafed through the folder, then read it in detail. He had no idea what to expect, but in fact at first sight the report was neutral, neither offering him any encouragement nor disquieting him further.

Miranda's fingerprints had been found everywhere in the vehicle; as with the close relatives of all police officers her prints were on file for comparative purposes. There were few other dabs, surprisingly few perhaps, but a great many smudges. And, attached to the upholstery of the passenger's seat a couple of dark brown hairs had been found. The interesting thing about these was that they had been dyed; originally they were blond. Miranda was a natural brunette, and had no need to dye her hair. Of course, the hair could have come from someone to whom she had given a lift at any time in the past, but the colouring of the hair was odd, to say the least; in Thorne's experience, few blondes chose to be brunettes. It was a tenuous thread . . .

He put the file to one side, and picked up the next. Over the past couple of days work on the Farling case had concentrated on any possible connections between Parker and Burwash and any other known criminals who might have been in league with them. The only report of any consequence seemed to have come from an off-duty detective-constable who had been having a drink in the public bar of the White Swan outside Colombury.

The constable had shown some initiative, Thorne thought, by casually mentioning the murder at the Farlings. Everyone present had promptly seized the opportunity to air his or her view, but it was Madge, the barmaid, who had commented on a couple of customers who had seemed to think that the poisoning of the Judge's Dobermann had been a great joke.

The constable had been about to leave, but he hastily ordered another pint, and remarked, untruthfully, "I'd not heard about the dog. Tell me. Who thought it was a joke?"

"Oh, just a couple of chaps," Madge said.

"Willie Burwash and Bert Parker, perhaps?" the constable asked, speaking softly so that others in the bar didn't hear.

Madge hesitated. "Yes," she admitted at last. "But it wasn't them that did it," she added quickly.

"Did they know who did?"

"No, I don't think so. They were just laughing, and saying it served the old bugger right—and pity it hadn't been him; that sort of thing. They meant the Judge," she explained unnecessarily. "Just in fun, you know."

"No names mentioned at all?"

Madge hesitated again. "Well, they did say some guy

called Tony Mull'd be as pleased as Punch about it, but that was all. They didn't suggest he knew anything."

Thorne finished reading. "That's a most interesting report," he said. "The constable deserves a medal—or a drink, at least. Tony Mull, eh? It could be a lead, as you say, Sergeant. Do we know of any connection between him and the Parker-Burwash double act? How are they after a weekend in jug, anyway?"

Abbot grinned broadly. "They've realized they've got rights, and they've seen a solicitor, sir. As far as I can make out, even he didn't think they'd any hope of getting away with it—at least with the vandalism charge. And with their records—well! The break-in and the killing are a bit different, sir."

"I appreciate that. Still—"

"As to possible connections, sir, there's no doubt they could easily have met Tony in jail. He's doing six years, most of it still to go, if you remember. I checked the locations, and they were all in the same place for quite some time."

"Of course I remember Tony Mull—and his blasted family," Thorne said sharply. "It was my case, by Jove. What's more, Mull was up before Farling. He knifed a police officer who damn near died. He was lucky to get away with six years, in my opinion. Not like old Farling to be so lenient."

"The Mulls may not have considered it lenient, sir. They might have thought a spot of their own back was in order. They're a very clannish lot."

"Um—" Thorne paused. "Well, what's the latest on the blasted mob?"

"Well, Ma Mull still runs a stall in Oxford market, and keeps the family together, as it were. Eddie gives her a hand, when he's not otherwise engaged in a spot of petty larceny or receiving, or worse, much worse. He's only done one stretch so far, but there's no doubt he's deserved more. He's a thoroughly bad lot, and I'd say he'd be fully prepared to use violence—if he's not done so already."

"He's not the eldest, is he?"

"No. That's John, but he doesn't live at home any more. He left after his pa fell in the river and drowned. Rumour had it John pushed him when they were both drunk, but nothing was proved—and now John's said to be going straight. But I don't believe it. He's a Mull."

"John!" Abbot looked up in surprise as Thorne repeated the name. In fact, the Superintendent had recalled that John was the name mentioned by the barman at the King's Head. A common name, certainly, but he remembered also that John Mull was tall and dark, and the thought that the Mulls might be connected with Miranda's disappearance had suddenly hit him. "A spot of their own back," as Abbot had said—both on the judge and on the police officer who'd been largely responsible for sending one of them down.

"A pleasant family," Thorne said finally, shaking his head in disgust. "Who else is there?"

"Well, Tony's in jail, sir, and Pete's in a Borstal. That only leaves young Ronnie. He's a kid—twelve or thirteen —but he's in and out of trouble already."

"Five sons," Thorne said thoughtfully. "But according to Stephen Crispin one of the characters at the Farlings' was a woman. Crispin may be a novelist, but I can't believe he made that up."

"No, sir. But Eddie's got a wife, and so's Tony. They all live with Ma Mull."

"That's right," said Thorne. "Got their names?"

"Eddie's wife's called Gloria, I think, sir, and Tony's married to a local girl called Nettie."

"I see." Thorne sighed. He would have to interview the Mulls, and think about John Mull and look into his whereabouts. But first he needed to have another chat with Burwash and Parker; after a weekend in which to consider their positions they might well be more communicative. And he must also go to his bank, and talk to Ian Dawson, which meant a trip to London. The day wasn't long enough.

As Thorne debated his next move, a woman police officer came in with a message. The owner of a high-class jewellery shop off the Marylebone High Street had just reported that some pieces of silver he had bought on Saturday were on the stolen property list. It seemed likely that in fact, they were a few of the items Sir Leo Farling had said were missing.

"What efficiency!" Thorne said with heavy sarcasm. "That robbery took place last Wednesday. With all these computers and whatnot, those items should have been in a list reaching every police station by Thursday at latest, and circulated to likely buyers the same day. No wonder our clear-up rate's so low."

But secretly Thorne was pleased. At least one of his problems was dealt with. He could pay an official visit to London to see the jeweller, and call on Ian Dawson afterwards. Burwash and Parker would have to wait a few hours, but while he was away the recent movements of all the Mulls could be checked.

Quickly he issued orders and made the necessary arrangements with the Met. If possible he wanted to avoid wasting time on a courtesy visit to the Yard; in fact they seemed only too happy that he should go directly to Marylebone. Pressure of work, even with their overlarge staff, Thorne supposed acidly.

Half an hour later he was sitting beside Abbot in the police car, a purposeful expression on his face. Abbot was thankful that the Superintendent looked reasonably cheerful.

"I want to go to my bank first," Thorne said.

"No need, if it's cash you want, sir. I've got plenty."

"It isn't."

Thorne didn't explain, and Abbot drove dutifully to the local branch of Barclays Bank and parked outside it on a yellow line. He had just seen a rather attractive traffic warden, and was hopefully waiting for her to threaten him with a ticket, when Thorne reappeared.

"All right, Sergeant," he said. "Get going."

It was the last remark Thorne made for miles. Slumped in his seat, he stared, unseeing, through the windscreen. He was frowning fiercely and once, without making any sound, he mouthed the words, "Mad! Mad!"

It made no sense. Miranda had sold the little yellow Mini with which she had been so delighted, and the proceeds had been paid into their joint account. If she had been short of money, he could have understood her selling the car; it was her own, and she could get cash without drawing on any of their joint money. But no. Seemingly lack of funds was not the reason. She had withdrawn nothing—not a penny—from their account, which Thorne had half feared she might have denuded. It was, he thought resentfully, one more damned mystery.

The cheque had been paid in at lunch-time on Friday, when the bank had been busy. Thorne had been lucky in that one of the tellers had remembered the transaction; it was unusual for such a large sum to be paid into the Thornes' account over the counter. Further, the depositor had not been Mrs. Thorne, but a tall, dark, good-looking man. The girl stared at Thorne, suddenly anxious. "Everything was in order, wasn't it?"

Thorne had been forced to reassure her, even to comment that he didn't mind who paid money in, providing they drew none out. But he did mind; he minded very much. He had begun to hate this mysterious character, who was always with or near Miranda.

Abbot cleared his throat loudly, and the Superintendent started, as if he had been asleep. By now they were on the outskirts of London, and traffic was heavy.

"To the local station first, sir? You said you'd fixed it so we didn't have to check in at the Yard. But it's getting on for the lunch-hour."

Thorne readjusted his thoughts. "Yes, you're quite right. The local station, Sergeant. Then we'll find a pub." He could phone Ian Dawson from a pub, he thought, and wondered what he would do if Dawson were uncooperative. After all, the man was primarily Miranda's friend and colleague. He scarcely heard Abbot's "Very good, sir."

But by the time they had reached central London and Abbot was threading his way along Oxford Street, Superintendent Thorne's mind had sharpened. They spent fifteen minutes at Marylebone Lane Police Station, signed a receipt for some pieces of Sir Leo Farling's silver, refused lunch and a somewhat reluctant offer of an officer to accompany them during their inquiries, and persuaded the Station to park their car. Then Thorne hurried Abbot along Wigmore Street to a pub he knew from his London days.

"Order us a couple of pints and some hot food," he said. "I'll leave you to choose, Sergeant. I'm going to phone Headquarters."

The telephone was where Thorne remembered it, in a corner of the saloon bar, and comparatively secluded. He dropped coins in the box, dialled Dawson's number and waited impatiently. In fact, a girl answered almost at once. He gave his name, and expected to be told that Mr. Dawson was in conference, or out of the office, or otherwise unobtainable.

Instead, there was no delay at all; Dawson came on the line immediately. "Hello, Thorne. Nice to hear from you. Where are you? Is Miranda with you? I've been trying to get in touch with her."

"I'm in London, not far from your office. I'd like to come and see you this afternoon if it's at all possible."

"Yes. Indeed." There was a clear question in Ian Dawson's voice but he didn't hesitate. "What time would suit?"

Thorne thought rapidly. Food. The jewellers. Getting from there to Dawson's office. "Say about three?"

"Okay. See you then." The slightest pause. "You'll be alone?"

"Yes. About three. Thanks."

Thorne hung up the receiver before he had to face any other queries, found more money, dialled again. Over his shoulder he saw Abbot pick up two tankards from the bar and carry them over to a table by a window. He spoke quickly, authoritatively, then listened. He was shaking his head in disgust as he joined Abbot.

"Well, they've learnt something this morning, but I doubt if it's much use. Ronnie, the youngest Mull, has been boasting to his schoolmates. One of them seems to have thought the officers had come to arrest him—guilty conscience, no doubt—and he gave the game away. It was Ronnie who put that lighted cigarillo in the Judge's pocket at St. Giles' Fair. He recognized Sir Leo from his brother Tony's trial."

Abbot suppressed a grin. "Wretched brat," he said. "I'm thankful it wasn't you he spotted at the Fair, sir. He probably knows you by sight, too."

Thorne took a long gulp of beer, and wiped his moustache. "I dare say. And he'll know us better if he goes on this way. It looks as if he's getting set to become a real villain."

"Anything else, sir?"

"Not yet. The officers who saw them say that Eddie and the two young women were polite, too polite, and cagey as could be. They didn't seem surprised by the visit, but I don't suppose that means much. No one has seen John yet, or old Mrs. Mull."

"And of course Eddie's got a cast-iron alibi?"

"He was in bed, he says, asleep and dreaming the dreams of the innocent." Thorne finished his beer as the food arrived. "Still, it's early days yet," he added absently, wondering if he could face the mound of shepherd's pie the waitress had placed in front of him. It wasn't that he disliked shepherd's pie. On the contrary, as made by Miranda, it was one of his favourite dishes. That was the trouble; this wasn't Miranda's pie. It wasn't what he would have chosen for himself.

To avoid embarrassment he forced himself to eat a certain amount, and toyed with the rest. Abbot pretended not to notice, but he was worried. He had been called aside on arrival at Headquarters a few days ago, and told the Chief Constable wanted to see him. Surprisingly, Midvale had treated him almost as a senior colleague, whom he could safely take into his confidence. It had cost the Chief a lot of words to say so, but it appeared that he wanted Abbot to keep an eye on Superintendent Thorne —in the nicest possible way, of course.

And there was no doubt that Thorne was not his normal self—though any bad temper or unusual indecisiveness could readily be accounted for by the worry of Miranda's continued absence. The Superintendent had never been an easy man to work for, but Bill Abbot, to do him justice, had always got on well with him—and, on the occasions when they had met, with Mrs. Thorne. Abbot had no wish to spy on his superior, but he would certainly help him if he could.

"Apple pie, sir?" he asked. "Or would you rather be pushing off now?"

Thorne looked at the large clock over the bar, and checked it with his watch. "Let's go," he said. "According to the report the Swains live over their shop, so they should be in."

William Swain and Sons was a small establishment, but obviously a long-established firm of jewellers, which also carried on a discreet pawnbroking business. According to the reports, William Swain was dead, but the shop, owned by his two sons, had an impeccable reputation. David Swain, the older son, whom they interviewed, was most upset by what had occurred.

"It was my fault, my carelessness," he admitted at once, as he took the two police officers into the office behind the shop. "I should have checked the latest list, but I had a heavy cold—you can hear it still—and my brother was away, and, well, I just—" His excuses tailed away.

"Had you done business with the vendor personally before?" Thorne said, mentally taking back his earlier harsh thoughts about police inefficiency.

"No." David Swain shook his head. "But he was well dressed and well spoken, and we're—we're not exactly the kind of place that someone would normally come to with stolen goods. I can't remember it ever happening before. I know that's no excuse," he added. "I should have checked the list."

"Tell us exactly what happened, Mr. Swain."

"Well, this man came in, put the silver on the counter, and said, 'How much for these, would you think?' I looked at the pieces and gave him a price, and he said, 'Fine,' and that was that. I wasn't thinking very clearly, you know, Superintendent. It was this damned cold and it was a simple sale and purchase—nothing to do with the pawn-broking side of the business."

"But you'd still need a name for your records, your accounts—" Thorne began.

"I know, Superintendent, I know," David Swain interrupted. "And it was forthcoming. He was a very plausible gentleman. He gave me his name, address, phone number. Here they are. I've written them down for you, but they're no use. I've had time to check them by now, and of course they're phoney."

"All right, Mr. Swain, I understand," said Thorne. "But I expect you'd know the man again." He nodded at Abbot, who produced a sheaf of photographs.

"I might, but I doubt it," said the jeweller grimly as he looked through the file. "Anyway, he's not one of these, unless—"

"Unless?" Thorne prompted.

"There's one here that's a possibility, though I couldn't swear to it. He doesn't look so—so self-possessed and sure of himself in the photograph, but it isn't a very good photo, is it?"

"No," Thorne agreed as he studied the print that Swain had handed to him. It was not, he had to admit, a good likeness of John Mull, Eddie's elder brother. "Could you describe him for us?" he asked. "Was there anything special you noticed about him?"

"No. I told you, Superintendent, I wasn't at my most observant that day." The jeweller shook his head; he had begun to have second thoughts. "I could easily be wrong about that photograph," he added. "All that I really remember was that the chap was tall and dark—"

"And good-looking?"

"Not that I noticed."

Swain frowned, obviously puzzled by the Superintendent's question. Sergeant Abbot, who could have enlightened him, had swallowed an expletive and was staring at his shoes. He had followed Thorne's train of thought with ease. The man who had been seen on more than one occasion with Miranda Thorne had been tall, dark and good-looking. Could it conceivably have been John Mull? To Abbot it seemed extremely unlikely, but . . .

"What I don't understand," the jeweller continued, "is why the stolen items should have been brought so openly to a shop. I'd have thought any experienced thief would have taken them to a fence."

"I expect that's just what happened to most of the stuff that was taken," Thorne said. "But these were a few small and valuable items, weren't they? It wasn't a bad gimmick, taking them to a first-class store like this, and hoping no one would be thinking about stolen goods. After all, it worked. And if the man had thought you were in the least suspicious, he could just have walked out, couldn't he?"

"Yes," sighed the jeweller. "I only wish he had."

CHAPTER 14

Superintendent Thorne avoided the doubtful-looking lift and climbed the uneven stairs. He was breathing heavily by the time he reached the fourth floor. This was not what he had expected at the offices of a literary monthly magazine which, though admittedly of somewhat limited appeal, was reputable and flourishing.

The solid door with its brass plate announcing "Ian Dawson Ltd." gave a somewhat different impression, however, and once inside Thorne revised his previous judgement. The rooms were small and well furnished, and apparently equipped with the latest technology. The receptionist who greeted him was operating a word processor, and another girl was studying the screen of a microfiche reader. The visible staff seemed to be fully occupied and all the signs suggested confidence and efficient management. Dawson, who, it turned out, was conferring with the receptionist, came forward to greet the Superintendent.

"Hello!" He wrung Thorne's hand. "I'm awfully glad you called. Come along to my inner sanctum. It's a bit early for tea. What about coffee?"

"Thank you, yes."

Thorne had no recollection of Dawson as such an exuberant character, and sensed that the big man's seeming joviality concealed the fact that he was somewhat ill at ease. He wondered why. Then, as Dawson waved him into his office and he was confronted by the view over the City to St. Paul's Cathedral he could momentarily think of nothing else. He stood and gaped.

"Yes—magnificent, isn't it?" Dawson said. "It strikes everyone the same way the first time. I should have moved out, and this building should have been pulled down years ago, but I've been fighting a running battle with the bureaucracy. I think if we had to move I'd sell the business." He laughed and gestured Thorne to a comfortable leather armchair. "How are you? It's some time since we met. And Miranda? How—how is she? Not too well?"

"Why do you ask that?"

A tap at the door and the entrance of a girl with a tray of coffee and biscuits saved Dawson from an immediate answer. They went through the formalities—How do you like it? Cream? Sugar? Biscuit?—but inevitably they eventually ran out of small talk. There was a lengthening silence.

Dawson cleared his throat. "You never said how Miranda was."

"I don't know," Thorne said bluntly. Conscious of time passing, of Bill Abbot waiting for him in the car, of the need to get back to Kidlington and cope with the pile of files that was undoubtedly accumulating on his desk, Thorne knew he couldn't fence with Dawson any longer. If he were to get Dawson's assistance he must take the man into his confidence.

"I don't know where she is," he repeated bleakly, and told Dawson as much as he thought necessary. He concluded, "I thought—I hoped *you* might know something about her. She was probably due to send you a puzzle—"

Dawson was shaking his head. "I've no idea of her whereabouts, but I did get a crossword from her this morning, with a note. It asked me to pay the cheque into her account." He gave Thorne a long, searching glance. "That was why I was trying to get hold of her. I knew there was something wrong even before you phoned."

"Why?"

"Perhaps I exaggerate. I should have said 'unusual,' rather than 'wrong.' Let me try to explain." Dawson gave an apologetic smile. "As you know, I publish one of Miranda's crosswords almost every month. Naturally, I have a couple of reserves in case she's ill or away or something, but normally I receive a puzzle in the first week of the month before it's due to appear. I've already received October's puzzle. So why should I get another one from her this morning? And why pay the cheque into her account, instead of sending it to her home as usual? The obvious explanation was that she was going away—on holiday? To have an operation, perhaps?—but, if so, I'd have thought she'd have said so."

"So that's why you asked me if she was unwell?" And when Dawson nodded, Thorne added, "Perhaps she *is* going away, right away. I wouldn't know. But she's given no sign of being ill." Thorne heard the break in his voice, and silently cursed his feelings.

Instinctively, Ian Dawson was careful to avoid showing his sympathy. He opened a desk drawer and made a business of finding Miranda's crossword and note. He glanced at them and passed them to Thorne, who took them, studied them for a minute and gestured hopelessly.

"It's Miranda's writing. What else can I say? Have you got the envelope?"

"Yes. I kept it, because there are one or two odd things about the enclosures, Superintendent. Here it is." He passed it over.

Thorne glanced at it. Again Miranda's writing. Mailed at Oxford Main Post Office on Saturday.

He looked up at Dawson. "May I keep these papers? You can make photocopies, if you like. You said there were oddities—"

"Yes, Superintendent—two in fact. First, the left-hand side of the new puzzle is almost an exact repetition of a puzzle we published a couple of months ago. This means we couldn't possibly use it—as Miranda would know perfectly well." Dawson made a hopeless gesture. "So why send it in?"

Thorne's experience and instinct told him that Dawson

had provided him with an important piece of information —if he could interpret it. "And the other thing?"

"Well, Miranda's always meticulous. I've never caught her out in a false reference or a misquotation or an impossible anagram. I'd trust her a hundred per cent." Dawson spoke earnestly, leaning forward, his eyes on Thorne's face, intent on impressing him with the significance of his words. "But look at Nine Down, Superintendent. The clue is 'Othello's Zenda,' and the solution, if you can call it that, is 'Rescue.'"

"What should it be?"

"God knows! These cryptic crosswords, as they're called, are meant for intelligent, well-read people, but they're not meant to be unreasonably abstruse. And this clue and its solution don't make sense. Before you told me that she'd—disappeared, I thought she might be ill, and had sent in a draft by mistake. It was the only acceptable explanation I could come up with immediately. Now—" Dawson paused, smiling a little tentatively.

Thorne interpreted his hesitation accurately. "Now—now you've thought of something else. Tell me—even if it seems far-fetched."

Dawson grinned ruefully. "It certainly does, but I suppose it's the crossword mentality—I'm an addict myself. You see, I thought that if Miranda were trying to send some message, 'Rescue' would be a plea for help. Zenda, after all, suggests prisoner. Othello—the Moor, the husband who wrongfully suspects his wife: that I don't understand. Unless perhaps she's being kept prisoner by someone called Moore? But, as you say, it's far-fetched—"

George Thorne was not stupid, but his mind didn't work in the same way as Dawson's, and it took him a minute to absorb what he'd been told. He had seen *The Prisoner of Zenda* on television, and he had read (or been forced to read) Shakespeare's *Othello* at school a long time ago. He could think of no one called Moore.

But Thorne knew he was being offered a lifeline—an

explanation that was just possibly credible. He grasped at it avidly, as his last hope.

Common sense told him that Miranda—driving away with her luggage, enjoying herself on a carousel at St. Giles' Fair, drinking in Woodstock, buying books in Blackwell's, selling her car, and all this without any obvious signs of coercion—had made it abundantly clear that she was a free agent.

But this crossword had to be significant. Apart from the impossible clue and its implications, the fact that half the puzzle was a repetition couldn't conceivably be accidental.

Dawson looked doubtfully at Thorne, and then said, "Please don't take offence, but it did occur to me that, if the whole thing isn't a product of my warped imagination, then one of the points Miranda might be trying to convey is that—well—that, like Othello's wife, she should be trusted."

"Yes. Maybe." Thorne pulled hard at his moustache, not noticing the pain he was inflicting on himself. "All I know is that I must find her and talk to her."

He repeated this to himself, again and again, as he thanked Dawson and said goodbye, as he returned to an anxiously waiting Abbot, and as he was driven back to Kidlington. He must find her. He must.

In Oxford, it was getting dusk as Stephen Crispin was leaving University College. He came out of the Porter's Lodge to hear a girl's voice, "Sign the petition. Please. Please sign. We've hundreds of signatures, as you can see, but we always need more. Please sign."

She was pretty, seventeen or eighteen, Crispin reckoned, and the street lamp suddenly went on and picked out red lights in her hair that reminded him of Lucy. He grinned at her. "What's it for?" he asked.

"Not what. *Who.* No, *whom,*" she said, and laughed at her own pedantry. She had taken Crispin for some kind of lecturer or professor. "Though perhaps even that's not quite accurate. It can hardly be for poor Jack Taylor, can it, now he's dead? You do know about Jack Taylor?" she asked.

"Sure. Who doesn't? The chap who was sentenced for killing his girlfriend because he thought she'd been unfaithful to him, then hanged himself in his cell before his appeal came up. It was a *cause célèbre*—just for a week or so, as I remember."

Crispin had lost interest in the girl, and made to move on. She barred his way, angry at his dismissal as trivial of something she considered vitally important. She wasn't going to let him go so easily.

"There was no proof," she said. "The evidence was all circumstantial, and the confession the police got out of him he withdrew later."

The girl was beginning to annoy Crispin. "Taylor had a fair trial, and he was found guilty. Anyway, he's dead. The affair's over, done with. So what are you petitioning for?"

"It's to send to the Home Secretary. To demand a retrial. To clear his name, for his family's sake."

"Oh, all right!"

Crispin didn't give a damn about the Taylor case, but the girl was so insistent it was simpler to sign than argue. He scrawled his name where the girl pointed, but received no thanks. Instead the girl said, "One day you might be grateful if people got up a petition for you. You never know with the police."

Crispin scowled at her and pushed past, wishing now that he had refused to sign the stupid document. He hurried across the High Street, and started up New College Lane, deserted at this hour, not long before dinner. Lucy was picking him up late, and they intended to have a meal and then go to a party. He had to get back to his flat to shower and change, but he had plenty of time.

He forgot the girl and her petition as he strode up the narrow, winding lane. His thoughts were on the evening ahead, which promised to be fun. He paid no attention to the soft, padding footsteps behind him, not even when he reached a particularly shadowed and tortuous part of the lane. Not even when the footsteps quickened, came up beside him.

What a dumb bastard, Eddie Mull thought, as he got an arm-lock on Crispin and forced him up against the wall. A dumb bastard—but, he reminded himself, dumb bastards could be dangerous. He wondered if he should waste this one, finish him off and be done with it. But that could be dangerous, too.

"What did you tell the police?"

At once Crispin recognized the voice on the phone, the cold, threatening voice, and he became stiff with fear. "I —I don't know what you mean," he said weakly.

"Don't give me that fucking nonsense. You went to Kidlington, the sods' Headquarters. We know. We've been keeping an eye on you."

"I had to go. I couldn't refuse."

"So what did you tell the fuzz?"

"Nothing! Nothing at all!"

Crispin's scream of denial was abruptly curtailed as Eddie Mull, without relinquishing the arm-lock, seized him by the hair with his other hand, and banged his face against the wall. Blood streamed from Crispin's nose into his gasping mouth. It was hard to breathe and the pain was intolerable. His knees buckled, but Mull held him upright.

"I warned you," Mull said.

"I know. I've done nothing. I told them nothing. I swear it."

"Then why have they got on to me?"

"I don't know!"

Mull shook him, and Crispin swallowed blood. A girl rode up the lane on a bicycle, but didn't give them a glance. Mull hesitated. He could hear voices coming closer, laughing voices, male voices.

"For the last time, Crispin."

"For the last time, I swear to God I told the police nothing. They showed me photographs—and I said I didn't recognize anyone."

Against his will Mull believed him; the creep was too scared to lie. But if not Crispin, who? Burwash and Parker wouldn't dare, and anyway they'd implicate themselves. "Keep it that way, or else—" he said venomously.

Without waiting for an answer, he banged Crispin's face against the wall again, and Crispin felt a tooth break. He spat it out as Mull let him go, and slithered down the wall into a crumpled heap. Never before had he met real physical violence; some bullying at school, the odd youthful scrap, but nothing like this. He lay as he had fallen, listening to the retreating steps of his attacker.

Then two young men, with the girl whose petition Crispin had signed so reluctantly, rounded the corner. There was a moment's pause while they wondered if he were merely drunk, but the girl recognized him and they saw the blood. Crispin muttered that a man had tried to mug him, and had only been prevented by their approach; he didn't care if they believed him or not. In fact, they couldn't have been kinder. He refused the police and the hospital, so they did their best to tidy him up, supported him as far as Broad Street, and saw him into a taxi.

Back in his flat Stephen Crispin went straight to the shower room. He stared at himself in the mirror over the washbasin and failed to recognize his own face. Dark blood was still trickling slowly from his nose. His mouth was swelling. The broken tooth had cut his lip, or perhaps it had been a rough stone. His skin was criss-crossed with small scratches, some of them still oozing blood. Gingerly he touched his nose; by some miracle it seemed unbroken. Then suddenly his stomach heaved and he turned quickly to the toilet to vomit into the pan.

When Lucy Farling arrived she found Crispin in bed. He had managed to clean up his face a little, remove his bloodstained clothes, and put on clean pyjamas, but his appearance, if anything, looked worse than before, as the bruising began to show. Lucy was horrified. He told her the story of the mugger, and at once she demanded that he call the police.

"No, Lucy. No. What's the use? They'd never find the chap."

"They might. Someone might have seen him hanging around."

"So what? I couldn't identify him. I had my face to that blasted wall all the time." Crispin was growing annoyed. He wished she wouldn't persist. The last thing he wanted was for the police to take an interest. He could hear his voice whistling through his broken tooth, and it didn't improve his temper, but at least it was better to feel angry than afraid. He made an effort to smile at Lucy; none of it was her fault, and he shouldn't take it out on her.

"Darling, it looks worse than it is," he said placatingly. "What I need now is a good strong drink—and you to stay the night to look after me. I don't need a doctor or any stitches, but tomorrow I'll see my dentist. And, please, let's forget the police."

Superintendent Thorne and Sergeant Abbot, the policemen who would have been most extremely interested in what had happened to Stephen Crispin, were still on their way back from London. It had been an almost silent journey. Abbot had hoped that the Superintendent would discuss the case, as he often did on such occasions, if only to clarify his own thoughts. But this evening Thorne had hardly spoken. He seemed totally preoccupied.

As they approached Kidlington, however, he moved restlessly in his seat, shifting his weight as if to ease his limbs. Once he sighed heavily. Abbot glanced sideways at him. Then Thorne coughed, and Abbot seized his chance.

"Sir, about John Mull," he said. "Are we going to pull him in?"

"John Mull?" said Thorne. "No. We haven't really got anything against him, have we? That man Swain would never be able to make a positive identification."

"So this trip to London has been something of a waste of time, you'd say, sir?" Abbot decided to risk a leading question.

Thorne paused for a moment, then he said, "Waste of time? On the contrary, Sergeant. I hope it may prove to have been of great importance."

If this remark surprised Abbot, he was even more astonished when, on reaching their Headquarters, Thorne immediately got out of the car, saying, "Right. I'll see you in the morning, Sergeant. Good night."

Abbot stared after the Superintendent as Thorne crossed the parking lot, got into his own car and drove straight off at speed. Maybe it was a bit late for the promised interviews with Burwash and Parker—they could certainly wait till morning, but at the very least Abbot had expected the Superintendent to make a token visit to his office to check over any reports that might have come in during the afternoon.

It was unfortunate that the Chief Constable happened to witness the incident, and speak to Bill Abbot. The Sergeant would gladly have shielded Thorne, but he was too taken aback to lie effectively, and Midvale was inevitably left with the impression that Superintendent Thorne was becoming less and less reliable.

CHAPTER 15

"If he must go with you, I'm coming too," Lucy Farling said firmly the next morning. "Can't you see he's not fit enough to be by himself?"

The two uniformed police constables who had been

sent to collect Stephen Crispin exchanged glances. "We didn't know anything about the mugging, miss. It wasn't reported. But I assure you Mr. Crispin will be perfectly all right with us," the older of the two said. "Maybe our medical officer could have a look at his face."

Lucy swore in a way that shocked the senior constable. "What I want to know is why?" she said. "Why? You might think Mr. Crispin hasn't been trying to help the police all he can. If this is how you treat honest citizens, then God knows what you do to criminals. After what he went through yesterday, Mr. Crispin ought to stay in bed. Do you realize what time it is?"

"Yes, miss. It's eight-fifteen. Detective-Superintendent Thorne wishes to see Mr. Crispin at nine, and we wanted to make sure—"

"—that the Superintendent wasn't kept waiting!" Lucy glared contemptuously at the officers and repeated flatly, "Okay. You win. But you can damn well wait till we're ready—and so can your blasted Superintendent."

The senior constable hesitated, then decided that it was pointless to argue further, especially with a judge's daughter. "Fair enough, miss," he said at length. "I'll wait here and help Mr. Crispin dress." Turning to his colleague, he said, "You go and keep an eye on the car." He took the other man's arm and murmured in his ear as he led him to the door, "Get on the blower and tell them the situation." Headquarters, he thought, could sort out the mugging business, and this Miss Farling, when they got there.

But Lucy hadn't finished. "It's absurd," she said, turning to Stephen. "You've told that man Thorne all you know. Darling, if you don't want to go—"

"Lucy, I'd better."

Stephen, who had been silently listening to her exchange with the police officers, was still in his pyjamas, though Lucy had been dressed when the doorbell rang. His face hurt like hell—he'd had no opportunity to shave, and he doubted if he could—but until the arrival of the police he had been feeling slightly improved. Now he hardly knew what to think, but he guessed what Thorne wanted. The authorities still believed that he could help them to identify the woman thief. This time it was vital he should convince them that they were wrong.

Eventually, he found himself sitting in the back of the police car, Lucy beside him. They held hands, but didn't speak. At the Headquarters of the Thames Valley Force they were received politely, and shown to a waiting-room. Coffee was brought for them, though Crispin had difficulty in drinking it quickly.

At five minutes to nine Sergeant Abbot came in. "Mr. Crispin, Superintendent Thorne will see you now." They both stood up, and he added. "Alone, Mr. Crispin."

"No!" said Lucy. "What is all this, Sergeant? Why are you treating my fiancé as if he were some kind of criminal? He's told you all he can about that business at my father's house. What more do you want?"

Abbot said nothing. He merely looked at Crispin, and made a slight negative movement with his head.

"Lucy, please. I think—" Crispin began, his swollen mouth making his speech slurred.

"Nonsense," Lucy laughed. "Why shouldn't I come with you? All right, Sergeant, lead the way."

Abbot, who had been warned by the Superintendent not to make an issue of Miss Farling's presence, led them along a series of corridors, remarking, "The Superintendent's seeing you in his office, rather than an interview room," as if this were a considerable concession. Lucy made no reply.

In Thorne's office, Abbot set chairs for them opposite the Superintendent's desk. At nine o'clock Thorne came in. He had been up half the night, puzzling over every clue of the crossword that Miranda had sent to Dawson. He had arrived at no startling conclusions, but he was convinced that Dawson was right. Clearly, Miranda was trying to send some kind of message. Whatever appearances might suggest, she hadn't walked out on him voluntarily; somehow she had been tricked, deceived, forced into her behaviour. But by whom? The only remotely likely suspect seemed to be John Mull, who had still not been located, but Thorne couldn't see him in the role.

Thorne's mind was half on how he was going to persuade the Chief Constable that the new evidence provided by Dawson was significant, so that Miranda's disappearance could become a matter of official police priority, and only half on the couple in front of him. He forced himself to concentrate.

Crispin's guess had been accurate. The Superintendent was hoping to bully him into making a greater effort to identify the woman Carter had almost captured; it had been part of the process of intimidation to bring him into Headquarters so abruptly. Lucy Farling's presence was a nuisance, but the mugging could be helpful.

"Miss Farling. Mr. Crispin." Thorne nodded at them. "I gather you've been in the wars, Mr. Crispin. In fact, I can see you have. How did it happen?"

It was the last question Stephen Crispin had expected. He stuttered, whistled through his broken tooth, and started on his story. Repetition had given him confidence, but almost at once Thorne held up his hand.

"You say this girl stopped you and asked you to sign this petition. Has it occurred to you she might have been deliberately delaying you?"

Crispin looked up in surprise. "Good God, no! She was one of the group that came to help me."

"What sort of petition was it? Any cause you'd ever heard of?"

"Oh yes. It was to ask the Home Secretary for a retrial of the Jack Taylor case—the chap who hanged himself in his cell—so as to clear his name for his family's sake." He hesitated. "I must admit I thought it was a lot of nonsense —after all, the affair's over and done with—but the girl was persistent."

Taylor's death had been nothing to do with Superintendent Thorne, but it was not one of his cases on which he liked to dwell. "Go on, Mr. Crispin," he said. He let Crispin complete his story, then commented, "And this mugger, as you call him, took nothing."

"No, undoubtedly he would have done, but he was interrupted, as I said."

"Describe him, please, Mr. Crispin."

"Well, he took me completely by surprise, but I got the impression he was tall and strong. I never got a chance to see him properly. He came up behind and banged me against the wall and—"

"Obviously very efficient," Thorne murmured, as if to himself, "except that he never managed to steal anything. Odd."

"Superintendent, what *is* the point of all this?" Lucy could contain herself no longer. "Surely you haven't brought Mr. Crispin all this way in his state just to question him about a mugging, when you know perfectly well you're never going to catch the guy."

"Oh, I hope to, Miss Farling. I really do," Thorne said mildly. "Now, Mr. Crispin, what about his voice?"

"Er—he didn't say anything."

"What? He didn't threaten you? He didn't warn you that if you told the police all you knew about the killing and the burglary at the Farlings', or made any identifications, you'd be for it?"

Sergeant Abbot coughed hurriedly. The Superintendent was bending the rules again. And how on earth had he jumped to the conclusion that the mugging was not what it seemed? From his expression, Stephen Crispin was asking himself the same question.

"Mr. Crispin," Thorne said sadly, "look at the timing, as you yourself describe it. If your story were completely true, it would mean that the girl with the petition must have collected her two friends, and all three must have positively hurried after you, to arrive at just the right moment—after the mugger had had time to hurt you, but before he'd had time to take anything, even your watch. Really, it's not credible, is it? Doesn't it look as if the so-called mugger was more anxious to hurt you than to steal anything?"

Crispin had no choice but to bluster. "Are you calling me a liar, Superintendent?"

Thorne stared at him. "Yes," he said bluntly. Then: "But I sympathize. In your place I'd probably lie in the same way. However, I've got sense enough to know it's a stupid thing to do. And you should know that too, Mr. Crispin. The man who's threatening you, or his associate, has already committed one murder. So far he's been content with beating you up a little, but don't kid yourself—he'll kill again if it suits him. There's no future—no protection —in going along with his demands. His doubts about you will grow as we get closer to him, and—"

Thorne stopped speaking. Stephen Crispin's face had gone a dirty grey, so that the cuts and bruises showed up as especially livid marks. He was making strange, guttural sounds at the back of his throat. Suddenly he cried, "Sick!" and clamped a hand over his mouth.

"Take him, Sergeant. Quick!" Thorne snapped.

Abbot was already on his feet. A big, strong man, he had no difficulty in half carrying Crispin from the room. The sounds of retching grew faint.

"You—You—I hope you're satisfied!" Lucy turned on Thorne. She was incoherent with anger, and if the desk hadn't separated them she would have hit the Superintendent. "Can't you see Stephen's dreadfully upset? It's not just being physically attacked. It's the shock. And you —you practically pull him out of bed, get him here, bully him. I—I'll report you. I know Philip Midvale personally, and I'll tell him what a shit you are."

Thorne's manner became formal. "That's your privilege, Miss Farling," he said. He got up, opened the door that Abbot had hooked shut behind him, and signalled to a

Woman Police Constable who had been waiting outside. He turned back to Lucy. "If you'll excuse me now, Miss Farling. This officer will show you the way out."

"I'm not leaving this place without Stephen, and without seeing your Chief Constable." Lucy spoke with determination.

"This officer will arrange everything for you, Miss Farling, if you'll go with her." He nodded to the WPC, who was one of the older and more experienced of the women constables at Headquarters. He knew she would cope with Lucy and her tantrums better than he could.

Lucy glared at Thorne as she went. Thankfully he closed the door behind her, but he heard her voice float back as she walked away along the corridor. "God, that man's a bastard! I'm not surprised his wife's left him."

Later it occurred to George Thorne that this was the moment when things started to go wrong, and his hopes of clearing up the Farling case quickly began to evaporate. Waiting for Abbot's return, he started on the files that had come in yesterday and overnight, but the memory of Lucy Farling's remark made it hard to concentrate, especially as nothing he read seemed of any special relevance or assistance.

Jean Haule had retracted the alibi she had given her brother and Willie Burwash for the night of Carter's murder, but this had been inevitable once the two men had admitted to being near the Farlings' property at the vital time. Old Mrs. Mull was in a private room in a hospital in London, about to have an operation, and Eddie had been trying to borrow a large sum of money. John Mull's whereabouts were still unknown. Nettie Mull, Tony's wife, was pregnant. Generally, the Mulls' fortunes appeared to be at a low ebb, but . . . What did any of this matter?

Thorne swore softly to himself, and Abbot's return provided a welcome diversion. "Crispin's okay, sir. I got him there in time, but he only retched. He didn't puke properly."

"Where's he now?"

"Helping to make up an Identikit picture of the woman thief, but he's not helping much. He keeps on contradicting himself, so the job's practically impossible."

"Is he faking?"

"In my opinion, yes, sir. At any rate, he's not trying. I'm afraid you didn't scare him enough, sir."

Thorne sighed. "Right. I'll see Burwash and Parker. You've had them brought over? Good. Then, afterwards, I'll have another go at Crispin. Get him ready to be wheeled in while one of the other jokers is with us—it doesn't matter which. I'll give you a nod."

"Yes, sir." Abbot departed and Thorne waited. He looked at his watch. He had put in a request to see the Chief Constable, and thought that by now he should have heard from Midvale's secretary. Wondering if Miss Farling had got in ahead of him, or if she had changed her mind, he smiled sourly.

Burwash was ushered in. He was surly and uncooperative, but he stuck by his story that he knew nothing about the Farlings' burglary or the killing of Carter. Thorne made him go over the events of the night step by step, and time after time, waiting for inconsistencies, but he could detect none. Reluctantly he accepted that he was getting nowhere.

"Is it Eddie Mull you're scared of, Burwash?" he asked suddenly.

Burwash's body tensed, but he managed to look scornful. "Why should I be scared of Eddie Mull? I don't properly know him. I shared a cell with his brother, Tony, one time. So what?"

"You'd prefer to serve a murder sentence, rather than squeal on Eddie? Is that it? Or was it John who shot Robert Carter?"

"I don't know what you're talking about." Burwash had forced himself to relax.

"Don't you?" Thorne paused, thinking that Burwash had reacted to Eddie's name rather than John's.

"No, I bloody well don't. I know my rights and I've seen a solicitor, and he tells me you'll never make a murder charge stick—not even a manslaughter—not with the evidence you've got, nor no accessory rap neither. As for Eddie Mull, or any of the Mulls, I don't know nothing about them, but I'm not going to help you frame them, if that's what you're trying on."

It was a long speech for Burwash, and there was a ring of truth in it. Certainly Burwash sounded confident, in spite of a weekend in custody. Thorne cursed the lawyer who had given his client such advice, accurate though it might be.

The interview with Parker was no more rewarding. Told to sit, the man settled himself comfortably, so that his bottom just rested on the edge of the seat, his legs, crossed below the knees, stuck straight out in front of him and his head was pillowed on the back of the chair. Thorne ignored the insolence.

He went through the same sequence he had followed with Burwash, and with similarly negative results. The mention of the Mulls quite clearly made Parker nervous, but brought a swift denial that he knew anything of their activities. As a last resort, Thorne nodded to Abbot, who got up and left the room, to return a few moments later with Stephen Crispin.

Crispin looked pale and composed, until he took two steps forward into the room and stopped, staring at the back of Parker's head. His eyes widened, his mouth opened and he swallowed hard.

Parker, aware of something happening behind his back, swung himself round, his face tilted up to confront Crispin. "Who's this, then?" he said.

Crispin gave him one horrified glance and turned his

gaze to the floor. Thorne got up and moved swiftly round the desk to stand at his side. Parker, finding himself uncomfortable, resumed his previous position. For a moment they formed a static tableau. Then Thorne gave a nod, and quickly murmured some instructions to Abbot.

Parker, shaking his head in apparent bewilderment, was escorted from the office. Crispin was seated in the chair Parker had occupied. Thorne returned to his place behind the desk, and Abbot, who had disappeared for a moment, returned with a file that he opened in front of the Superintendent.

Thorne said, "You recognized Parker, Mr. Crispin?"

"If—if that was Parker sitting here, then no. I've never seen him before."

"You thought he was someone else? Someone you've seen? Now, who did Parker remind you of? A woman, perhaps?"

"Nobody! I was just startled to find someone with you."

Thorne leafed through the file in front of him. Then, seemingly, he changed the subject. "These Identikit pictures aren't much good, Mr. Crispin."

"I'm sorry."

"Can't you do better? Surely you saw what colour hair the woman thief had."

"Brown. I said it was brown."

"Not red? Are you sure? Mr. Crispin, I put it to you that the woman had short red hair, and was not unlike Parker. That was why you were so startled—"

"No! No! I don't know what you're trying to do to me, but it's not right."

"Are you sure you can't identify the woman you saw on the floor of the Farlings' hall, Mr. Crispin?"

Crispin took a deep breath. It made his face hurt, and reminded him of the danger of his situation. If he told the police, they would arrest the woman and the man would keep his threat. If he didn't tell them, if he continued to deny all knowledge— He didn't believe what Thorne had said earlier. "No," he said stubbornly. "No. I'm sorry. It all happened so quickly."

Thorne and Abbot exchanged glances. "Okay," Thorne said. "Sergeant Abbot will take a statement from you, Mr. Crispin. Then we'll send you home in a car—with Miss Farling; I imagine she's still around—or we'll take you to your dentist, if you like. And if you change your mind, let us know."

Thorne spoke curtly, but politely. He was annoyed, but he thought he understood Crispin's situation. The identification he had been on the verge of getting probably wouldn't have stood up in court, but at least it would have assured him he was on the right track. He'd handled Crispin badly, and missed his chance. He kicked himself.

The phone rang. If the Superintendent was not busy, the Chief Constable would see him at once.

Thorne went along the corridor hopefully. But there was bitter disappointment in store for him. Lucy Farling had complained. Midvale was not in a good temper, and totally uninterested in Miranda's crossword, and what might be deduced from it. He had no time for such niceties, and he impatiently dismissed Thorne's request that his wife's voluntary departure should be a matter for the police. What the Chief Constable *was* interested in was a report on Thorne's progress with the Farling case. He seemed unimpressed by what Thorne had to say. Action was what was needed. And he hinted—though it was no more than a hint—that if the Superintendent was so occupied with his personal affairs that he couldn't concentrate on his work, he might consider some sick leave.

Thorne contained his anger, but only just. He left the Chief Constable's office in a frustrated fury, feeling as if, like Stephen Crispin, he had come up against a stone wall.

CHAPTER 16

"So what d'you want now? Haven't you sods got anything better to do than come after poor peoples like us?"

"Gloria Mull? Mrs. Edward Mull?"

"That's me."

She stood just inside her hall, and spoke through the half-open front door. She was ready to slam it at any moment. About five foot seven, with long legs, slim hips and full breasts, her figure might have made her a candidate for a Miss World contest. But her figure would have been her only qualification. Her thick red hair was cut like a man's, her skin was white, her features pointed. She looked what she was—tough, shrewd, unscrupulous.

A fit mate for one of the Mull boys, Superintendent Thorne thought as he introduced himself. He had come to interview Gloria Mull, to turn the house over in search of the Farlings' stolen property and the gun that had killed Robert Carter, to take Gloria in for questioning. Thorne had no real hope that anything incriminating would be found on the premises; the Mulls were much too wary for that. And he had made sure that Eddie Mull was out of the way before he launched his raid. The Chief Constable had said he wanted action, and action he was going to get.

"Sure, I know you. You're the one that helped send our Tony down," Gloria Mull sneered. "And what d'you want now?" she repeated. "And why half the Thames Valley Force with you?" She made a disparaging gesture towards the three police cars lined up in front of the house, and the officers getting out of them. "Scared to come alone, Superintendent?"

"There are some questions I have to ask you, Mrs.

Mull," Thorne said. "And we propose to search your house. We have a warrant. Please let us in."

Already neighbours' heads were appearing at windows. Passers-by were stopping to stare. A half-dozen small children, who should presumably have been in school, were inspecting the police cars. A trio of obviously unemployed youths had sauntered up. Thorne was delighted at the interest he had caused, if only because it induced Mrs. Mull to acquiesce without a fuss.

"Eddie at home?" he asked conversationally, as Gloria Mull led him and Abbot into the front room.

"No. He's gone up to London to see Ma. She's ill. Something wrong with her guts."

"Too bad." Thorne sat down without being asked. "And the rest of them?"

"As if you didn't know where Tony and Pete are," Gloria Mull said bitterly as she perched herself on the arm of a sofa. "And I bet you know about the others, too. Anyway, Nettie's minding the stall in the market. Ronnie's in his room watching telly. He's got a cold which is why he's not at school, if you're thinking of reporting him. And, like I said, Eddie's gone to the Smoke."

"What about John?"

"Haven't seen him for months."

Thorne could hear his men moving, heavy-footed, about the house, opening and shutting drawers and cupboards, calling to each other. In accordance with their briefing, they were making no attempt to conduct the search quietly. Gloria Mull couldn't fail to hear them too.

"If they do any damage I'll sue," she said. "What the hell are they looking for, anyway?"

"Sir Leo Farling's silver. The gun that was used to shoot Bob Carter, the Farlings' houseman."

There was a small silence. Gloria Mull's face was expressionless but her foot, which had been tapping the air, was suddenly still. A uniformed inspector opened the door, glanced into the room and nodded to Thorne, as if in confirmation. As the Superintendent expected, this was a cue for Gloria Mull to explode.

"You've not found anything. There's nothing here to find—not unless you brought it with you. You bleeding shits—"

Thorne waited until she had stopped cursing, then gave her the formal warning, which she chanted with him derisively. "I must ask you to come to Headquarters with us now, Mrs. Mull," he said. "There you'll be charged."

"What with?"

"Robbery with violence? Accessory to murder?" Thorne shrugged. "We'll think of something, Mrs. Mull."

Gloria Mull gave a loud, long laugh. "You really mean it, don't you? You really mean to pin this Farling business on us."

"That shouldn't be too difficult, Mrs. Mull, not with an eyewitness."

Sergeant Abbot looked up sharply, terrified at the thought of the next indiscretion Thorne might commit, but the Superintendent merely stood up. "A woman police officer will assist you to find a coat and pack a few things, Mrs. Mull. You'll need to arrange about Ronnie, too, I dare say. Perhaps a neighbour—"

Ten minutes later Abbot was driving Thorne back to Headquarters. Apart from a little cannabis hidden in a stuffed toy on Ronnie Mull's bed, nothing at all incriminating had been found, and Abbot wondered why the Superintendent seemed so pleased with himself. It was lucky for Abbot's peace of mind that he couldn't know what Thorne was thinking.

While Gloria Mull was stoutly maintaining her right to refuse to answer any further questions till she had seen a solicitor, Bert Parker and Willie Burwash had appeared briefly in the local magistrates' court, and been remanded on bail. Temporarily free, they had returned to Jean

Haule's house, buying a case of beer en route to help them celebrate.

It was Jean who had arranged their bail, and when she returned home from her dress shop later in the day, she was furious to find them both drunk—or well on the way to it. She lost her temper, and told them to clear out, but they merely laughed at her.

"You fools!" she shouted. "You're out on bail, that's all. You've not had your case heard, let alone dismissed. You've not got away with anything, even a fine or a suspended sentence—as if you could expect to, with your records," she added scornfully. "The police are collecting evidence, just as they said and, when they've got it, they'll charge you with that killing."

"There isn't any evidence. We were never in the house." Parker seemed to think the whole affair a joke.

"That won't save you. If they can tie you up with whoever shot that chap—"

"The solicitor said—" Burwash began. He had difficulty in articulating the word "solicitor," and repeated it several times.

"Anyway, they can't—tie us in with it, I mean. Not as long as we keep our mouths shut." Parker was even more drunk than Burwash. He burped loudly. "And we'll do that all right. Eddie'll kill us if we don't."

"Eddie?" Jean, who had been standing by the kitchen table, pulled back a chair and sat down heavily. She looked from one man to the other. "Oh God!" she said in a whisper. "Eddie Mull. You *are* mixed up with the Mulls. It was them that did for—"

"Forget it, Jean! Forget what Bert just said." Burwash was suddenly sober.

"How the hell can I forget it? Those Mulls'll stop at nothing. You've put us all at risk—me, the kids. I'll never forgive you. Never!"

"Forget it, I said, love." Burwash leant across the table, and seized Jean's wrist, twisting it till she cried out. "Bert never mentioned Eddie Mull—or any of the Mulls. Got it!"

"Yes." Jean massaged her wrist as Burwash released it.

"That's okay, then. Have a beer, if there's one left."

The doorbell rang, and the three of them became quite still for a moment. It rang again, one long continuous shrill peal. Upstairs a door opened, and a child's voice said, "Ma, someone at the front door." Jean steadied herself.

"All right. Go back to your homework. I'll get it."

Without a glance at Bert or Willie, Jean went into the narrow hall. Automatically she cast an eye at the mirror as she passed, and patted her hair. Her wide, frightened eyes surprised her. She opened the door a little, carefully, wishing she had a chain on it.

She had assumed it was the police, but a solitary man in jeans stood there, with a leather jacket and a motor-cycle crash helmet. She couldn't see his face because the darkened visor was down. He put a hand on her chest, pushing her against the wall, and the front door wide open. He slammed it behind him.

He lifted his visor. "Parker and Burwash. They here?" he asked quite casually.

"In—in the kitchen."

"Who else?"

"In the house? Just me and my young son and daughter, upstairs, doing their homework."

By now Jean had guessed the identity of the helmeted visitor, and she moved defensively to the foot of the stairs as if to bar his way. Eddie Mull grinned sourly. "Oke. You join them while I have a little chat with your men."

Jean fled, and Mull went through to the kitchen. He didn't waste words. He took one look at the empty beer cans littering the place, and spat on the linoleum among them.

"Right," he said. "Which of you two angels shopped me? Or was it both of you? Don't bother to lie, 'cos I'll find out, and whoever did it is going to have a nasty accident."

"It wasn't us. We never shopped you. Honest," Parker said hoarsely.

Mull seized him, pulled his head back by the hair, snapped open a flick-knife and put it to Parker's throat.

"For God's sake! I swear it, Eddie. You tell him, Willie."

Willie did his best. "—and that's the truth, Eddie. Our lawyer sprung us, and we're out on bail. Jean put up the money. That Superintendent mentioned you when he talked to us, but we swore we knew nothing. We're not fools, Eddie. Once we shopped you, we'd be for it ourselves, wouldn't we? Can't you see that? We're in this together now."

"How right you are." Mull released Parker, shut the knife and slid it back into his pocket. "If it wasn't either of you, it was Crispin. I had the pigs in my house this morning. They turned the place over from top to bottom and they took Gloria in. She managed to get a word to young Ronnie. They say they've a witness. They could be lying, but she said they sounded bloody sure of themselves."

"Crispin, of course. It must be Crispin." Parker leapt at the chance to point the finger elsewhere. "Lucy Farling's boyfriend. It was in the papers. He saw the shooting."

"What wasn't in the papers was that Gloria got her hood pulled off, and he got a good look at her."

This was news to Parker and Burwash, but they weren't slow to realize the implications and take advantage of them. Burwash whistled loudly. "So that proves it. That must be it, Eddie, you see. Crispin's a menace to all of us."

"Yeah, Bert. To all of us, and especially to me and Gloria. I thought I'd scared the little shit enough to shut his mouth, but I could have been wrong. Anyway, he's got to be wasted, and quick. And I can't do it. As I say, he's special to me and Gloria and the fuzz'd guess at once."

Parker and Burwash avoided each other's eyes. They were fully prepared to use violence; indeed, they'd done so before—but only in the heat of a moment of danger, to save their own skins. Neither of them had ever gone out to kill in cold blood. They didn't want to now.

"But, Eddie, you don't mean we should—" Parker began to protest.

"Why not?" Eddie Mull gave them no choice. Nor did he leave them in any doubt about what he expected. He gave them Stephen Crispin's address and phone number, plus a description. "If it can be 'accidental,' so much the better—save a lot of trouble," he said dispassionately, as if he were discussing arrangements for a party. "Push him under a bus, or pinch a car and run him down. He lives in North Oxford, and there are some nice quiet roads around there. But get it done, and get it done quick. Tomorrow. Otherwise— Remember your woman, and the kids upstairs, as well as yourselves. If anything happens to Gloria —well, I think the world of my Gloria. Tomorrow."

Eddie Mull pulled down the visor of his crash helmet, and stalked out of the kitchen. The two men heard the front door slam, and sat in silence till Jean came slowly down the stairs.

"What do we do?" Parker asked urgently.

"Just what Eddie said," Burwash replied. "We've got no choice, Bert."

Superintendent Thorne was having supper in his kitchen when the phone rang. He had heated a tin of soup, and was following this with bread and cheese and pickled onions. Propped open in front of him was a book; the *Complete Works of Shakespeare,* which Miranda had won as a school prize. Thorne was reading *Othello* slowly, studying every line. He even had a pad of paper beside him in case he wanted to make notes.

"Yes?" he said, his mouth full of cheese.

"Superintendent Thorne? This is Sergeant Whittaker, sir, in the control room. A report on Edward Mull's just come through. You said you wanted to be informed if there was any action."

"Go ahead, Sergeant."

"He returned home at seven-thirty, sir. He was wearing a suit and looking very—very snazzy, sir, according to the officer keeping observation. He stayed home for under an hour. Came out wearing jeans and a leather jacket and carrying a crash helmet. He collected a motor bike, and drove to Colombury, where he went directly to the house of Mrs. Jean Haule. He was inside for about thirty minutes. He then returned home, where he is now."

"Thanks, Sergeant. Did he know we were behind him?"

"Apparently he gave no sign of it, sir."

"Good. He may be going out again, possibly to pay a call on Stephen Crispin. You'd better warn whoever's watching Crispin. Phone me if there are any other moves."

"Will do, sir."

Thorne washed up his supper dishes, made himself a mug of instant coffee and returned to *Othello*. In fact, Eddie Mull didn't leave his house again that night, but as the evening wore on, the Superintendent found, to his annoyance, that the message had disturbed him and he could no longer concentrate on Shakespeare. His thoughts kept returning to the Farling case. The search of the Mulls' house and Gloria's arrest seemed to be provoking Eddie into action, which was what he had hoped for. He supposed the sudden call on Burwash and Parker had been to reinforce any previous warnings about squealing. If so, it was tacit confirmation that the two of them knew more than they'd admitted. After all, they'd been in the garden. They could have seen . . .

For a moment Thorne buried his head miserably in his hands. Then he straightened. This wouldn't do, he thought; it wouldn't get him anywhere. It was Miranda that mattered. He must forget Carter's death, the Farlings, Crispin, his work—and to hell with the Chief Constable. Nothing mattered but Miranda.

He thrust the Shakespeare aside. He was a practical man, not a literary type, but he knew he had a quick,

intuitive, logical brain. If that crossword meant anything
—and Miranda's handwriting had been firm and assured;
there was no question that she was ill—then it was a message. She was a prisoner, seeking rescue. Start from that
basis, Thorne told himself.

The obvious contradiction was that she appeared to
have gone of her own free will, but the detective in
Thorne had learnt to distrust contradictions, bits of a puzzle that didn't fit. He forced himself to consider what he
knew. He'd been over it all before in his mind, but this
time he drew his pad towards him and started to make a
list.

Miranda had been seen leaving the house by neighbours. Abbot had recognized her at St. Giles' Fair. She had
been to that bar at Woodstock, had bought books at
Blackwell's, had sold her car.

And suddenly Thorne saw a possible flaw in what he
and everyone else had accepted. No one who knew her
well had seen Miranda close to, had actually spoken to
her. Suppose—just suppose—it hadn't been Miranda, but
merely someone who looked like her, dressed like her, in
her clothes—impersonating her.

It would mean that she had in fact been seized by some
trick. Please God, she wasn't harmed! But why should she
be taken? For what purpose? No contact had been estab-
lished, no demands made. Therefore it was no form of
blackmail—and, as far as he could see, that left only revenge as a motive. The villain must be someone who bore
him a bitter grudge. Thorne shuddered at the implications.

CHAPTER 17

The next morning Thorne arrived at Headquarters early.
He had taken special care with his appearance and, if he
seemed a little tired and gaunt, he at least looked spruce
and well cared for. His shirt was clean, his shoes highly
polished, his moustache trimmed and he held himself pur-
posefully upright. Aware that at present his relationship
with the Chief Constable could reasonably be termed
somewhat strained, he wanted to give Midvale no excuse
for further suggestions concerning sick leave.

Besides, he knew that he would carry more authority if
he looked more like his normal self. During the last few
days he had had the impression that his colleagues, even
those who had originally thought Miranda's disappearance a good joke at his expense, had begun to treat him as
someone unpredictable, to be humoured, if not avoided.
But today he wanted their help, and he was determined
to get it.

He wanted the files searched for any of his cases in
which the defendant had threatened him, or might be
expected to bear him a personal grudge; he wanted particular attention paid to any females who had recently
been released from prison, or who had a name resembling
Moore. It would be an exacting, time-consuming task, he
knew, as there was no point in doing it unless it was done
thoroughly and carefully, and because some of the more
subjective criteria were not readily susceptible to com-
puterized search through the data banks. A great deal
would depend on his colleagues' goodwill, and their respect for him. What was more, if his orders were questioned, or if the Chief Constable heard of them, his effort
could be thwarted. Midvale was highly unlikely to sanc-

tion the work; yesterday he had made it only too clear that he had said his last word on the subject of Miranda—unless or until her body were found, Thorne supposed bitterly.

In the event, though there were some mild grumbles and an inability to give his request absolute priority, no one in Records seriously questioned it. Superintendent Thorne, hiding his relief, went to the canteen for a coffee and then to his office, to cope with his mounting paper-work—and to wait.

By ten o'clock that morning Eddie Mull had still not left his house, merely appearing in pyjamas and towelling robe to take in the milk. Later he had waved Nettie off to the market, and Ronnie to school. He opened the door to the postman, and stood on the step for a moment or two, as if sampling the damp, autumn air. Superintendent Thorne, informed of all this, finally decided to take action and have him brought in for questioning, and by ten-thirty Eddie was being driven away without protest in a police car.

At Kidlington he was shown into an interview room, and almost immediately Thorne came in, with Sergeant Abbot. Mull crossed his legs, and regarded them with mild contempt.

"I'm thinking of suing you for false arrest," he said.

"We haven't arrested you yet," Thorne said mildly. "We haven't charged you with anything. You're just helping us with our inquiries."

"It's on behalf of Gloria I'd be suing you."

"Hadn't you better wait and hear what she's told us?" Thorne didn't expect an answer; Mull was too experienced to fall for that old trick. "Why did you go to Jean Haule's last night?" he asked.

Mull showed no surprise. "So you've been having me shadowed, have you? Been tapping my phone, too?"

"Answer the Superintendent's question," Abbot said sharply.

Mull grinned. "I went to have a chat with Willie Burwash and Bert Parker. I thought they might be able to help me. After all, they were at the scene of the crime, as you call it, and maybe they'd tell me something they wouldn't tell you—something to clear Gloria."

"And did they?"

"No. They didn't see a damned thing. As you know perfectly well, they just peppered the old Judge's greenhouses and fled, the silly sods! Wanted to get a bit of their own back for the sentence he gave them, so they said."

"Don't you believe them?"

"Oh, sure. But greenhouses! I ask you! That's kid stuff."

"Like Ronnie?"

"Okay. Okay. I admit it. He admitted it. I tanned his hide real good for putting that lighted smoke in Farling's pocket. Stupid, that's what it was. It ain't going to help Tone none." He shook his head.

"And you?"

"Me? What d'you mean—me?"

Thorne didn't answer, and at length Mull said, "Oh, all right. I see what you're getting at. But, Superintendent, I'll tell you straight up. If you're thinking that Gloria and me broke into Farling's house to do him down for what he did to Tony, you're losing your grip. If we'd done it at all, we'd have done it for the goods. Silver mainly, wasn't it—good pieces? I bet it'd fetch enough to buy my poor old Ma all the specialists she needs. I might have been tempted." He laughed, but his words had carried conviction.

Thorne found himself accepting them, albeit somewhat unwillingly; Eddie Mull had had no thoughts of direct revenge, though doubtless he hadn't minded that it was Judge Farling's house he had decided to rob.

"Where's your brother John?" Thorne asked abruptly. "No one seems to know what's happened to him?"

"I saw him yesterday. First time for ages." The question didn't seem to faze Eddie. "He went up north after Pa had his—er—unfortunate accident, and we lost touch. He lives in Bradford—runs a clothes business there. But when he heard Ma had to have an operation he came down to see her. He's in London right now, staying in rooms near the hospital. He never got on with Pa, but he was always Ma's favourite. D'you want his address?"

Thorne nodded, though he guessed it was pointless. The Met would check, and John Mull would be there, an honest, respectable citizen, for whom the Bradford police would vouch in due course. He watched Eddie as he dictated addresses and phone numbers to Sergeant Abbot. At least, he thought, this should rule out John Mull as a possible kidnapper of Miranda—not that he had ever taken this theory very seriously.

Suddenly it hit Thorne that something was wrong. Eddie wasn't behaving in character; in fact, quite the reverse. He wasn't angry, uptight, wary; even his crack about suing for false arrest had been just that—something of a joke. For some reason, he seemed perfectly happy to sit and respond to questions, as if he regarded the whole operation as a friendly chat rather than a police interview. Why?

Thorne changed his tactics. "Now let's cut out the gags and get down to business," he said abruptly. "You realize you no longer have an alibi for the night Carter was killed, don't you, Mull?"

"How's that?" Eddie didn't appear worried.

"Your alibi—such as it was—depended on your wife, Gloria. However, as we can now place her at the scene of the killing, I don't imagine you'll want to continue to claim to have been with her."

"I was with her, all right. In bed. You prove otherwise, Superintendent."

"That's no problem."

Thorne spoke with a complacency that he didn't feel.

Eddie Mull was still smiling, superficially derisive, but the eyes that met Thorne's had suddenly become full of hate —or possibly fear. Before Thorne could judge which emotion was uppermost there was a tap at the door. Abbot got up and had a brief conversation with the officer outside, who handed him a note.

The Sergeant returned, his face expressionless, and gave the note to Thorne. Eddie Mull was pretending to look bored and uninterested.

Thorne read the note quickly, and felt sick. This was his fault. Angered by the Chief Constable's indifference to his personal problems, he had acted rashly, had failed to take sufficient precautions. And bloody Eddie Mull had been sitting there, laughing at him, secure in his alibi for one crime at least.

"Okay," Thorne said. "Have him put on a holding charge, Sergeant." He stalked out of the interview room.

Like Thorne, Stephen Crispin had woken comparatively early. He edged out of bed so as not to disturb Lucy, and went into the kitchenette to put on the coffee. His face hurt less this morning, though the bathroom mirror told him it was no thing of beauty—the bruising was by now a dirty green—but the dentist had made a good job of fitting a temporary cap on his broken tooth. On the whole, he thought, he looked interestingly ill rather than totally disreputable.

His appearance, however, was of secondary importance. The real problem was his conscience. He knew perfectly well that he should do his duty, and identify the red-haired woman. He was in no doubt that Superintendent Thorne knew that he could. Nevertheless, he remembered that cold, threatening voice on the phone, that ghastly experience in New College Lane, and he shied away from committing himself.

The smell of coffee was filling the small flat. Lucy was awake and calling to him. Crispin abandoned the inspec-

tion of his face, and thrust aside his thoughts. He went to
her.

"Why are you up so early, Stephen?"

"It's not really so early. It's getting on for nine and I've a
couple of coaching sessions this morning. I can't cut them.
Besides, I must go to the bank and there's a heap of other
things to do."

Lucy argued, but lost. Shortly after ten they left the flat
together, turning left along the road. Lucy's car was
parked in a nearby side street, and Crispin, who had only
a few hundred yards to go to his first appointment, walked
towards it with her. Hand in hand they strolled along the
pavement, and began to cross the road.

Thorne's instructions had been to follow Crispin's
movements, and keep an eye on him. Accordingly, one of
the officers in the unmarked police car which was parked
further along the road switched on his ignition. He didn't
hurry. He was facing the opposite direction, but he knew
he could turn at the next corner, and he had been told it
was preferable if the subject didn't know he was being
followed.

Willie Burwash, in the driving seat of a sleek white
Jaguar that Bert Parker had nicked a short time ago, and
the loss of which had not yet been reported, acted far
more rapidly. His engine was already running and, as
Lucy and Crispin came towards him, he was edging away
from the kerb the moment they stepped off the pavement.

"Now! Go!" Parker said urgently, and Burwash jammed
his foot down on the accelerator. The powerful car shot
forward.

Lucy was speaking and, absorbed in her words, Crispin
was unaware of the Jaguar racing towards them. The police officers were powerless to help directly, but the
driver, watching the scene in the rear-view mirror, thrust
his head out of the window and, perhaps unfortunately,
shouted a warning. Startled, Lucy and Crispin stopped.

By now the Jaguar was almost on them. Lucy screamed, and in the next moment Stephen Crispin used all his weight to push her out of the path of the car. She stumbled across the road, landing on her hands and knees in the gutter. As she looked back she saw the Jaguar strike Crispin, lift his body into the air, and throw it aside like a bale of hay. Sobbing, she staggered to her feet and went to him.

The police made an effort to intercept the Jaguar, but Burwash was determined to get away. With great skill he gave the police car a vicious side-swipe, spinning it around. Then he careened across the road, mounted the pavement, scraped along a low wall and shot away.

The police officers were unhurt. One jumped out and ran back to where Lucy was kneeling beside Crispin's still form. The other was on the radio to Headquarters, calling for an ambulance and describing the Jaguar and the two men in it.

He was a young officer, and his report was more excited and less formal than might have been expected from an experienced man. "Sure, I'd know the buggers again, one at any rate," he was saying. "They had woollen caps pulled over their heads, but I saw their faces clearly. They weren't expecting witnesses, certainly not us. Our try to intercept them came as a shock. The driver was dark, needed a shave. The other was freckled and gingery. And yes, it was deliberate, no doubt about it. They were out to get Crispin, and by the looks of it they did. Where's that damned ambulance? The girl? She's okay. Crispin pushed her out of the way, reacted very quickly, probably saved her life. Plucky little devil. He could have jumped for it himself and left her."

It was an edited version of this report that had forced Superintendent Thorne to bring his interrogation of Eddie Mull to such an abrupt end.

* * *

Thorne returned to his office in a furious temper. At once
he started issuing instructions. Find the white Jaguar and
go over it thoroughly. Arrest Parker and Burwash. Get
them identified by the officers in the police car. Then
charge them with attempted manslaughter—at least—
whatever alibis they produced. Bring in Jean Haule for
questioning. Keep in touch with the hospital where Crispin had been taken . . .

Thorne had not forgotten Miranda, but for the moment
he had forced her to the back of his mind. A steady flow of
material about his past cases was arriving, and he hoped
that among it would be a real lead. But he would have to
be patient. At least it was some consolation that the problem was not being neglected, that others were working on
it for him.

By late evening he had the satisfaction of knowing that
though much more detailed work would be needed before it could be put before the DPP, the Farling case was
virtually complete. The abandoned Jaguar had been
found, and Parker and Burwash picked up with very little
trouble. Bert Parker, confronted by his weeping sister,
and irrefutable evidence of his presence in the Jaguar,
had admitted everything. With some reluctance Willie
Burwash had done the same. They were fortunate that
Stephen Crispin, though badly injured, was expected to
live, and Thorne was confident that Crispin would at last
accept that silence couldn't buy him safety, and be persuaded to identify Gloria Mull.

It had been a long day. Thorne was tired by the time he
got home, his briefcase bulging with the first of the reports he had requested that morning. He thought he
would have a strong whisky and something to eat, and
then get down to sorting through them. Too late he remembered that the whisky was finished, and there was
very little food in the house.

However, a pleasant surprise awaited him. In the garage, which he had left shut but unlocked, he found a

basket containing groceries, some fresh salad vegetables, fruit, a couple of small casseroles and a bottle of Black Label. With it was a note: "Mary provided the food, but I'm responsible for the drink. Let us know how you are. Mary sends her love. Dick."

Blessing the Bands, Thorne let himself into the house. He left his briefcase in the sitting-room, put away the food, except for the casserole he intended to heat for his supper, poured himself a drink, and went to the phone. The least he could do, he thought, was to phone the Bands and thank them. He hadn't been in touch since the weekend, and he did have some kind of news of Miranda.

Mary Band answered the phone. Dick was out visiting a suspected appendix, but he'd be delighted that George had phoned. They'd both been worried about him, and about Miranda. Had he any news?

Thorne told her about Ian Dawson and the crossword. Repeated in cold blood, as it were, the clue and the interpretation Dawson had suggested sounded absurd. Mary tried hard not to appear discouraging, but clearly she was not impressed.

"So you think Miranda might be a prisoner of someone called Othello?" she asked doubtfully.

"No, no! Not Othello. Of course not." Thorne did his best not to let his impatience show. "Someone called Moore, perhaps. After all, Othello was a Moor. But of course that might be quite the wrong way to think of it."

"H'm. Difficult. I'll put it to Dick. He might come up with something. All I know about Othello is that he smothered his wife because he thought she'd been unfaithful to him."

They talked for another couple of minutes before Thorne repeated his thanks and rang off. The casserole wasn't yet ready, so he took another drink into the sitting-room and started to riffle through the reports he had brought home. Almost at once he came upon the Taylor case.

About to put it aside, Thorne suddenly sat quite still. Jack Taylor was dead, and no petitions would bring him back to life. Nor were they likely to clear his name. There was no doubt he'd killed his girlfriend. He'd been guilty as hell.

But he had smothered his girlfriend because he believed she'd been unfaithful to him.

George Thorne felt weak. Othello had killed Desdemona because of her alleged infidelity. But had he smothered her? Was it a true parallel? Had Mary been right? He leapt from his chair and ran to find the Shakespeare. His hands shook as he leafed through the pages.

Yes! There it was, as plain as anything, almost at the end of the play. Othello with Desdemona, and Othello says, "It is too late." Then the stage direction, *"Smothers her."*

In both cases, if you could call *Othello* a case, a woman had been smothered, as Miranda would have known. Quite apart from the media, he had himself discussed the Taylor case with her at the time and during the trial and when young Jack had hanged himself. Thorne told himself he must not jump to conclusions, but . . .

He sat, oblivious of his surroundings, torn between fear for his wife if she were in the vengeful hands of Jack Taylor's parents, and hope that he might soon find her.

CHAPTER 18

Though Superintendent Thorne had spent a large part of the night going through the reports that Records had provided, he had found no other lead. All his hopes were pinned on the Taylor connection, however tenuous that might seem.

Jack Taylor was only nineteen when he murdered his girlfriend. He was the only child of a respectable middle-class couple, his father the manager of a men's clothing store, his mother a beautician. Taylor himself had recently started work as a clerk in a bank, and had become engaged to an attractive girl he had known most of his life. He had no record, and his future had seemed routine and rosy—until, unfortunately as it turned out, the girl met another man whom she preferred.

It was a pathetic little story, and had only become a sensation when Jack Taylor hanged himself in his cell while awaiting his appeal. Superintendent Thorne remembered most aspects of the case perfectly. He could picture Taylor clearly—tall, dark, fairly nondescript—but he had more difficulty with the parents. He had interviewed them on several occasions during the investigation, and naturally they had been in court throughout the trial, but that had been some time ago and the impression he retained of them was vague.

At least one thing was in his favour, Thorne thought as he drove to Headquarters the next morning: the petition to the Home Secretary on Taylor's behalf provided an excellent excuse for inquiries about the present whereabouts and activities of the Taylor family.

But on reaching his office, Thorne found Sergeant Abbot awaiting him. Abbot looked unhappy and ill at ease, though Thorne was too preoccupied with his own thoughts to notice.

"Sir, the Chief Constable wants to see you at once."

"Okay. I'll be right along."

"Sir, he did emphasize the 'at once.'" Abbot swallowed tentatively. "I think it's about Mr. Crispin, sir."

"Crispin?" Thorne was instantly alert. "He's not died on us, has he?"

"No, sir. But Sir Leo Farling seems to have made a complaint." Abbot avoided meeting Thorne's eye. "To be blunt, sir, I think the Chief Constable's bloody angry, if you don't mind my saying so."

"He is, is he?" Thorne drew in a breath and blew it out.

"Right, Sergeant. I'll go along and see what he's angry about. Meanwhile, you start to think about the Taylor case, and collate all the available information on Jack Taylor's parents and family—even on any friends he had. I want as much as possible as soon as possible."

Abbot had the sense to show no surprise. "Of course, sir," he said.

They left the room together, Abbot bound for Records and the computer room, Thorne for the Chief Constable's office. Philip Midvale was one of those big, heavily built men who rarely permit themselves the indulgence of losing their tempers, but Abbot hadn't exaggerated. Today he was bloody angry.

He was standing in front of the window, hands clasped behind his back. He glowered at Thorne and made no attempt to return the latter's greeting. He gestured to a chair, but didn't sit himself. When he spoke his voice was hard and clipped.

"Superintendent Thorne, I want an explanation of the orders you gave and the actions you took that relate in any way to the attack on Miss Lucy Farling and Mr. Stephen Crispin yesterday. I gather that Miss Farling has escaped with shock and bruises, but Mr. Crispin is seriously injured. It seems to me you're lucky they weren't both killed."

"Sir, I regret that either of them was hurt, but there's one thing you must bear in mind. No attack on Miss Farling was intended. She just happened to be there. In my view, the attack was aimed entirely at Mr. Crispin."

"Just happened to be there, did she?" The Chief Constable was sarcastic. "And suppose half a dozen schoolchildren had just happened to be there, Superintendent?"

"Then I imagine that the attempt would have been called off, sir. The villains' aim was to—"

"I know what their aim was, damn it! And maybe you're right. Parker and Burwash might well have drawn the line at ploughing into a mob of children. But the thought of Miss Farling's death or injury didn't worry them."

"She's scarcely been hurt, sir."

"By chance, and only because Stephen Crispin kept his head and threw her clear. And what about Crispin himself, anyway? By bringing in the Mulls you set him up as a target. You bloody well knew there would be an attempt to kill him." The Chief Constable paused for a reply.

"I thought it likely, sir, yes," Thorne said. "That's why I had two officers watching him. After all, he is a valuable witness. He saw the actual shooting at the Farlings' house, and he could identify one of the intruders."

"He's denied that."

"He was lying. The fact that Mull wanted him dead confirms that he was lying."

"You know that's not necessarily so, Superintendent. It only confirms that Mull thought Crispin might be able to make an identification. Whether Crispin was in fact lying is quite another question. And, Superintendent, even if your supposition were correct, you had no right to treat a member of the public like a"—the Chief Constable searched for words—"like a tethered goat. Do you understand what I mean?"

"Stephen Crispin was in danger whatever I did, sir. My error, as I see it, was not to have him guarded more closely."

"Are you blaming the officers—"

"Certainly not, sir. Any blame is mine."

"Yes." The Chief Constable nodded abruptly. He crossed the room and sat down heavily. He looked at Thorne with an expression that was difficult to read. His anger had begun to dissipate.

"Superintendent," he said more quietly, "in all the circumstances I'm taking you off the Farling case."

"But, sir—"

"Thorne, at the very least your judgement was at fault. I understand and I sympathize with your situation, but since your wife left you you've not been totally reliable. Your mind's not on your work. You spend time—your own and other people's—which means the taxpayers' money, trying to prove the unprovable. Why on earth can't you accept the fact that your wife has left you? You won't be the first man—"

Thorne interrupted. "Are you suspending me, sir?"

"No, Superintendent. I'm merely ordering you to take some sick leave. And I'll give you a word of advice. Dick Band's a friend of yours, I know. Consult him, professionally. Perhaps he'll suggest a psychiatrist. I'm not making this official in any way, but until you get yourself back to normal you're not going to be much use to the Thames Valley Force."

The Chief Constable had spoken pleasantly but firmly. Now he stood up. The interview was at an end. Thorne concealed his anger. He said, "Sir," with the smallest inclination of his head, and walked out of the room, shutting the door quietly behind him.

For some minutes Philip Midvale continued to stare after him. It was absurd on the face of it, he told himself, but somehow there lurked at the back of his mind the feeling that it was his own judgement that was at fault and that he had done Detective-Superintendent Thorne a serious wrong.

For his part, Thorne returned to his office, cold, as if with shock. He sat at his desk and fiddled with the pens and paper-clips upon it. The phone rang, but he ignored it. Then he noticed the envelope on top of his in-tray. It was marked "Taylor."

A brief note from Abbot said that he had been sent out on another case, but the material in the envelope, though sketchy, was probably all that was available. Thorne glanced through it. Abbot was right; there wasn't much. After their son's death the Taylors had given up their jobs, and moved from the city. Their present address was unknown without further investigation. But Abbot had noted the name and address of an aunt who had visited Jack Taylor in prison.

Thorne's lethargy vanished; however remote, this was a lead, and he must act on it quickly—before the news of his supposed "sick leave" spread through the Headquarters. He thought for a moment. First, a letter of resignation. He typed it, signed it with a defiant flourish, addressed the envelope to the Chief Constable, and left it in his out-tray.

His second task was more difficult, and might prove impossible. He needed a weapon. As a detective-superintendent of the Serious Crime Squad, he had the right to draw arms without the authority of a superior, but only for a specific assignment. If he had already been posted as off duty, he wouldn't have a hope, and his request would be reported immediately. He had to take a calculated risk that the Chief Constable would not consider the matter extraordinarily urgent, or that the bureaucratic machine would take some hours to work.

The risk paid off. Half an hour later, George Thorne, no longer in his own thoughts a detective-superintendent, walked out of Headquarters, got into his car, and drove away. He had with him a standard issue Smith and Wesson .38 revolver.

He drove straight to Abingdon, to the address of Jack Taylor's aunt. Miss Dorothy Murphy lived in a neat semi-detached house, its front garden bright with flowers. It was close to the hospital, and Thorne was reminded of the agonizing night scarcely two weeks ago when he had been searching for Miranda, and of his relief when the body was not his wife's.

The front door was opened by a woman in her forties with a pleasant round face, blue eyes and fair hair. She wore a grey skirt with a white blouse, and somehow gave an impression that she was in uniform.

"Yes?" she said.

"Miss Murphy?" The woman nodded.

Thorne made no attempt at evasiveness. "Miss Murphy," he said. "My name is George Thorne. I wonder if you could spare me a few minutes to talk about your nephew, Jack Taylor, and his parents."

Dorothy Murphy inspected Thorne suspiciously. "From a newspaper?" she asked abruptly, and when Thorne shook his head, "What, then? If you're one of those wanting me to sign that petition about Jack, I've said I won't."

"No, it's not that." Thorne hesitated. He didn't want to give his rank—his former rank, he reminded himself—but he did need to establish some credentials. He spoke with perfect truth. "Miss Murphy, I was the police officer in charge of your nephew's case. I'm making some inquiries."

"Oh, I see! Then you'd better come in."

The sitting-room into which Thorne was shown was comfortable, if slightly shabby, full of flowering plants. Miss Murphy gestured to an armchair, and he found himself gazing at a wedding photograph—a tall, dark, handsome man, and a fair woman in a froth of white. Miss Murphy followed his glance.

"My sister, Myra, and her husband," she said. "Jack's parents, as I'm sure you know. She used to be sorry for me because I wasn't married, but I've had the best of it in the end. I've a nice house, and a career—I'm a nurse at the hospital—and no worries about children."

"But you were fond of Jack," Thorne said. "You visited him in prison."

"Fond of him, yes—but I didn't dote on him. They spoiled him, those two did, especially his father. Jack only had to throw one of his temper tantrums, and he got what he wanted. And whatever he did—" Miss Murphy stopped abruptly.

"Yes." Thorne prompted encouragingly.

"I—I was wondering. Would you like some coffee?"

"Please. I should love some."

Left alone, Thorne looked more closely at the wedding

print. It had been taken over twenty years ago, and had never been a very good photograph. The colour was exaggerated, making the couple look unnatural, like waxworks. Thorne found it impossible to imagine what they would look like now.

When Miss Murphy returned with two cups of coffee and a plate of biscuits, Thorne said, "I think you were going to tell me something, Miss Murphy—about something awful that Jack Taylor once did, something that his parents accepted, without making a fuss. Am I right?"

"Yes. You're very perceptive, Mr. Thorne." Dorothy Murphy sighed. "It was a long time ago. A neighbour's cat scratched Jack rather badly, and he seized it by the tail and threw it under a car. He was twelve at the time, I think. Myra was upset and wanted to punish him, but John blamed the cat. John had no sense as far as his son was concerned. He swore Jack never killed that girl, but of course he did."

"Do you know what the Taylors are doing now, Miss Murphy? You're still in touch with them, I take it?" Thorne held his breath as he waited for her answer, and relief surged through him when she nodded vigorously.

"Of course. After all, she is my sister, though we haven't actually met for ages. We talk on the phone occasionally. Not very often. John wanted to cut himself off from everyone, which is why they sold up and moved. I suspect she has to wait till he's out before she calls."

"I understand, and I'm sorry." Thorne sounded genuinely sympathetic.

Miss Murphy was talking more freely now. "It's more than just a shame. It's my belief she ought to leave him, but she won't. And yet I know she's unhappy. Who wouldn't be, buried away in that isolated farmhouse on Otmoor? It's all very fine for John. He was born and brought up there, but Myra—"

Dorothy Murphy went on for some time, but Thorne was no longer listening. The mention of Otmoor had been like a punch over the heart. Ot—moor. *Ot* hello, the *Moor.* *Otmoor*—the old four-thousand-acre marshy plain to the north of Oxford and east of Kidlington, surrounded by the seven "towns," really small villages—Charlton, Beckley, Noke, Oddington, Fencott, Murcott and Horton-cum-Studley—where the farmers and gipsies had waged three years of guerrilla warfare against the landowners in protest at the so-called "enclosures" in the early nineteenth century, blacking their faces and arming themselves with guns, billhooks and sticks to tear down fences and uproot hedges.

Thorne knew he had the truth. The setting was right. The pieces fitted. John Taylor was holding Miranda a prisoner on Otmoor, and his wife had been impersonating her. He remembered with satisfaction the revolver he had left in his car. All he needed was the address, and—

"Are you all right, Mr. Thorne. You look—" Miss Murphy smiled doubtfully. She had nearly said he looked dangerous. She told herself that she must have imagined it of this pleasant policeman.

"I'm sorry," Thorne apologized. "A touch of indigestion. I wonder—would you let me have the Taylors' present address?"

"Why, yes. Don't you know it? I'm sure it's on your files somewhere, so I might as well. But, Mr. Thorne—" Suddenly Dorothy Murphy seemed embarrassed. "I—I must tell you, though perhaps I shouldn't. You won't be welcome there. I gather from Myra—it's more what she doesn't say than what she does—that my brother-in-law has become a bit odd recently. Personally I think it's something to do with the whole thing being raked up again through this stupid petition. Anyway he won't have anyone in the house—and he's got himself some sort of gun, for protection, she says."

George Thorne's immediate instinct when he left Abingdon was to drive as fast as he could to a confrontation with John and Myra Taylor. Prudence prevailed. It was not personal fear that made him reconsider the situation, but fear for Miranda. If, as Miss Murphy had implied, John Taylor had become unbalanced, and surely in any case no completely sane man would have planned such a complex revenge for his son's suicide, then there was every likelihood that he would be prepared to harm—even to kill—the wife of the man whom he held responsible and therefore hated beyond reason.

Instead, Thorne drove home. He changed out of his office clothes, and put on dark slacks and a sweater, with crêpe-soled shoes. He forced himself to eat, and he made a pile of sandwiches and a flask of coffee, to which he added the remains of a bottle of brandy. He fetched his field glasses, and considered what else he might need, settling for some large-scale maps of the area, a length of rope from the garage and a sharp knife.

He had no real plan. He intended to locate the Taylors' house, and make a reconnaissance while it was still light. Depending on what he saw, he thought he might wait till dark, then break in. If he didn't find Miranda he had no idea what he would do, but by now he was beyond caring.

It was a long time since he had visited Otmoor, and he had enough sense to find an Ordnance Survey map before he set off. This lonely and desolate tract, the home of rumour and legend dating from the times of the riots, had changed a great deal in recent years. The people living there still had a local reputation for being "different," but the marshy areas had been drained, and were now mainly arable land. The increasing population had extended the seven "towns," but there were still many relatively isolated farmhouses. Cossing Farm, where the Taylors lived, was one of these, near the centre of the area, and close to the course of the old Roman road that ran from south to north across it.

Thorne found the Taylors' house without great difficulty; at least he found a rutted lane, with a derelict signpost which read "Cossing." He drove past and, as the ground rose very slightly, he parked in the gateway of a field, and got out of the car. Looking back, he could see three hundred yards away a square, brick house with some windows tightly shuttered, and two or three small outbuildings. He studied the scene through his glasses. There was little cover round the place, and he realized that it would not be easy to approach except in darkness. He returned to the car and settled down to wait, his thoughts on Miranda.

CHAPTER 19

Miranda Thorne stood and stared through the small gap and cracks in the shutters outside the window of her room, watching the afternoon light begin to fade. She was close to despair. Tomorrow would be Saturday, and for nearly two whole weeks—two dull but increasingly frightening weeks—she had been a prisoner.

She had no clear idea how she had got here, though she had a good idea where "here" was. But all she remembered was setting out to do some shopping. She had been disappointed when George had said he had to work and couldn't take her to St. Giles' Fair, but it had been a lovely morning and it was no part of her character to regret the inevitable. She had been in good spirits as she drove into the supermarket parking lot. It was early, and she had no difficulty in finding an area of vacant spaces. She parked her Mini in one of them, got out and turned to lock the door.

This was where memory began to fail. A car had drawn up in the next space, and suddenly two people were crowding in upon her. One was a tall man, presumably the character she now knew as John, the other a woman wearing a yellow suit similar to her own. She had caught the merest glimpse of them—she doubted if she would be able to identify them again—before a pad had been clamped over her face and, despite her struggles, she was bundled into their car. There had been no time, before she lost consciousness, to cry out, to shout for help.

The next thing she remembered was this room—her prison for a seemingly endless time. It was of moderate size and pleasantly furnished as a bed-sitting-room, with a comfortable armchair and a small desk. In one corner, behind a screen, was a wash-hand basin. Books had been provided and she had been encouraged—ordered, in fact —to work at her puzzles. She had no reason to complain of her surroundings, or of the way she was being treated.

No one had threatened her, except when she had been forced at gunpoint to make that dreadful phone call to George. Meals had appeared at regular intervals, well cooked and varied, with plenty of fruit and fresh vegetables. The room was kept at a sensible temperature and she had some of her own clothes; how they had been obtained she didn't know and this bothered her, though she was glad of them. In short, had she been an invalid or recuperating from a serious illness, she might almost have enjoyed the enforced confinement.

But Miranda was not ill. She was a prisoner, and she hated being shut in—shuttered—cut off from the world outside; she was only glad she was no claustrophobic. She had neither radio nor television, and was not allowed a newspaper. Above all, she missed her husband. She worried about him constantly, and was afraid for him, guessing that it was because of him that she was in her present predicament.

Her captors were not totally efficient. When in her room, they took great care to cover their faces with simple hoods. On the other hand, they spoke, both to each other and to her, and there was no indication they were attempting to disguise their voices. What was more, Miranda had found herself able to see outside through unnoticed gaps in the old shutters, and the view, though limited, had been sufficient to indicate that her gaol was located somewhere in the Otmoor area; the sound of controlled shooting in the distance served to confirm her suspicion, for she knew there was a rifle range a couple of miles north of Beckley.

Miranda's main complaint was that the days were passing with inexorable slowness, and that conditions had begun to deteriorate. She could wash, but she was unable to take a bath or shower. Worse was the humiliation of being forced to use a bedpan whenever she wanted to go to the lavatory. Without fresh air and exercise, she was beginning to sleep badly. And, as her hopes of rescue decreased —she wondered if Ian Dawson had thrown her carefully devised crossword puzzle into his wastepaper basket— her fears grew greater.

This was especially true now that she was sure some crisis was imminent. The previous night she had heard her captors shouting angrily at each other. She had caught her own name, and knew they were quarrelling over her. Then there had been the sound of a blow, a fall, followed a little later by a bout of hysterical sobbing. Had they been arguing about whether to kill her, Miranda wondered, about how to dispose of her body; clearly they couldn't keep her here for ever.

On the other hand, she argued, there was no way they could let her go. The hooded heads were all very well, but they must realize that she could recognize their voices and describe the room. The man had told her his name was John—though whether that was true or not she had no way of knowing—but he had once and obviously inadvertently called the woman Myra.

Sighing, Miranda leant her head against the window. "Oh, George," she whispered, "George, why don't you come and get me?" And for the first time since her abduction, Miranda Thorne wept.

* * *

It would be a gross exaggeration to suggest there was panic at the Headquarters of the Thames Valley Police Force when it became known that Detective-Superintendent George Thorne had sent in his resignation and at the same time, in defiance of all regulations, had drawn a pistol. Police business continued as usual, calmly and efficiently. Nevertheless, a ripple of excitement was running through the entire complex, and speculation was rife.

For once the Chief Constable was badly shaken. He blamed himself for not having foreseen how Thorne might react, but he wasted no time repining. He set immediate inquiries in motion, and it was not long before he learnt of Thorne's sudden interest in Jack Taylor and his family. From this it was easy to guess where Thorne might have gone. There was some difficulty in tracing the Taylors, but when Sergeant Abbot remembered Dorothy Murphy that problem was solved.

A uniformed inspector, with a sergeant and two constables, were personally briefed by the Chief Constable and very soon set off for Cossing Farm. Their mission was to warn the Taylors to be on their guard, as it was believed that threats had been uttered against them. The officers were to be suitably vague and make no mention of Superintendent Thorne. If the Taylors agreed, the sergeant would spend the night in the house, and the constables would remain outside. Meanwhile every effort would be made to trace Thorne's movements.

"Above all," Midvale had insisted, "we want to avoid a scandal. For our own sakes, for the reputation of the Force and for the sake of Superintendent Thorne. He has been under great stress recently, and I had ordered him to take sick leave. But I fear I misjudged the situation. He is—er—sicker than I thought. He must be found and given help."

Wary of coming upon Thorne unexpectedly, the police officers approached Cossing Farm with some caution, though the question of physical danger never occurred to them. In their police car they drove slowly down the rutted track, and stopped in front of the house. By now the daylight was beginning to fade, though the building remained in darkness.

The inspector got out of the car, followed by one of the constables, and started towards the front door. The driver prepared to turn the car. No one hurried. They didn't know that Myra Taylor had chanced to see them arrive, and run screaming to her husband.

John Taylor seized the shotgun he kept ready in the kitchen and ran up the stairs to one of the front bedrooms. Violently he pushed up the window. Then he leant out, making sure the gun was visible. He had always known that this might happen, that Miranda Thorne might be traced, and though he hadn't told his wife he knew precisely what he would do in this event.

"Get out!" he shouted. "Get away from here! You down there, you police. Get away from here, or—"

"Mr. John Taylor?" The inspector, startled, gazed upwards.

"Sir," the constable whispered urgently. "Look! He's got a shotgun."

"I'm John Taylor, and this is my property. You're trespassing. Get away, or I'll shoot."

The inspector stood his ground. "Mr. Taylor, please. There's no need to get excited. We just want to talk to you. If you'd let us in we could—"

"What the hell do you take me for? Some kind of fool? I know why you're here. It's because of bloody Superintendent Thorne. Tell him to go to hell. What's more, he'll find his wife's there ahead of him unless you get clear."

The inspector drew a sharp breath. "Christ!" he said. "I think Thorne was right. They have got his missus."

"What do we do, sir?"

"Get back to the car for now." He raised his voice. "Okay, Mr. Taylor. If you don't want to talk to us, you don't have to." The two police officers turned and began to walk away.

It was never clear precisely why John Taylor reacted as he did. The sergeant, who had got out of the car, certainly had moved around to its rear and was starting to open the boot. Maybe Taylor thought he was about to produce weapons. Whatever his reason, Taylor raised his gun and fired. It was a wild shot, and one pellet just nicked the sergeant's ear, but it carried conviction, and immediately changed the character of the encounter. The inspector and the constable sprinted to the protection of the car and threw themselves in. Then the police drove off down the track as rapidly as they could. The sergeant swore as blood poured down his face, while the inspector reached for the radio. It was only seconds before he was speaking directly to the Chief Constable.

By the time the car had come to a halt a safe distance from the farmhouse, the inspector had received his orders. They were to wait for reinforcements. Any vehicle leaving the premises must be stopped, but otherwise the Taylors should be left strictly alone. The Chief himself would be with them to take charge as soon as possible.

"And what about Superintendent Thorne, sir?"

A pause. An audible sigh. "Head him off if you get the chance. I suspect he's somewhere around. He's not at home and for the moment we can't trace him. Otherwise use your discretion and do your best."

"Yes, sir," said the inspector, swearing silently.

Thorne, of course, had witnessed the whole episode. He had been studying the ground around the farmhouse through his field glasses, working out the best approach route, when he saw the police car drive up. The subsequent events, while confirming his belief that Miranda was in the house, also increased his fears for her safety. Abandoning his decision to wait till dark, he determined to set off at once.

He knew it would not be long before his colleagues—erstwhile colleagues—returned in force. Shots at police officers represented a major emergency. John Taylor must be quite aware of this, and would be ready for them; in fact, all the shutters had by now been tightly closed. And an important part of preparing for an attack might, in Taylor's disordered mind, entail disposing of Miranda.

Thorne's mouth was dry as he thought of what might be happening at this very moment. He forced himself to concentrate. Gun, spare ammunition, knife. He wouldn't take the rope, but he slung the field glasses round his neck. Hastily he drank half his flask of brandy-laced coffee, and set off.

His object was to reach the farmhouse, to do his best to discover where Miranda was being held, and get inside—all this without being seen by the Taylors or encountering the police. It was a tall order. He knew his chances of success were slim, but he knew he had to try. At least he might create a diversion, and give Miranda a chance to escape. He was quite prepared to shoot to kill if necessary.

To get close to the house took him longer than he had expected. The land was flat and offered little cover, even to a crawling man. But at last, apparently unobserved, he reached the shelter of some sheds from which he could inspect the house closely.

It had seemed from the distance that all the windows were tightly shuttered, but in fact one—a small casement window of frosted glass on the first floor—was not, and remained slightly open. Thorne suspected that it gave on to a bathroom or lavatory, and wondered how he could reach it.

A ladder was the answer, and he found one in a shed nearby. Slowly and silently he maneuvered it into position, and at last he found himself beside the narrow window. The rest was easy. He used his knife to release the latch and climbed through on to a toilet seat.

Reaching back, he pushed the ladder to one side, and

heard it fall with a soft thud to the ground below. He saw with satisfaction that it lay alongside the house and didn't look as if it had just been put to use. Quietly he shut the window. No one seemed to have noticed his entry. Revolver in hand, he went to the lavatory door, eased it open and listened.

Apart from a patch of light coming from a half-open door along the passage, everything was in darkness. He could hear voices from inside the lighted room, but not what was being said. Then suddenly he heard a voice outside booming through a loud-hailer, and knew that he was no longer alone. The police had arrived.

"Mr. Taylor, this is Philip Midvale, the Chief Constable. Now, we don't want anyone to get hurt, so be sensible. Just throw your weapon out of the—"

The disembodied, distorted, persuasive voice continued, following the textbook rules for such situations. But inside the house Thorne heard a gasp of horror. The next moment the door of the lighted room was flung wide open and a woman dashed out. She was sobbing as she ran, along the passage and down the stairs, almost falling in her haste. She was of medium height, plump, with dark, curly hair, and she wore a bright red dress.

For a fraction of a second George Thorne thought it was his wife, Miranda. Then, with a spasm of revulsion, he realized it was Myra Taylor, in one of Miranda's dresses and with her fair hair dyed. He heard her running steps in the hall below, and the Chief Constable's voice cease abruptly as the front door slammed.

Now John Taylor was shouting, presumably from a window of the lighted room—something about kicking a chair, which made no sense to Thorne. He began to edge along the passage. He had no means of knowing Miranda's whereabouts, and he had decided to take Taylor from the rear while the man's attention was occupied by the police outside. He was almost by the open door when he heard a different distorted voice.

"John, this is Dick Band. Dr. Band. Your doctor. For God's sake, have some sense. Your wife's told us. Don't do this dreadful thing. What's the point, man?"

"I'll do it! I swear I'll do it. Unless you're all gone in two minutes, I'll kick the chair."

"All right, John, they'll go, and you and I'll talk." Band was obviously doing his best to sound calm and in control of the situation.

"There's nothing to talk about, Doctor. If you think I'm afraid to die, you're wrong. I'm not going to rot in prison any more than my Jack did. I'll kill myself, but I'll take her with me. Now, get out, the lot of you. I'm counting. One . . . Two . . .

George Thorne gritted his teeth. It wasn't the first time he had taken part in siege operations, but before he had had no personal involvement. This was different. He pictured the scene outside, the appearance of withdrawal, the hurried consultation, the Chief Constable's decision whether to attack or to wait, to use tear gas or try persuasion once more. Thorne himself had no such doubts. He was certain that John Taylor meant what he said, and that in the end, whatever action the authorities took, he would kill Miranda and then take his own life; probably this was what he had always intended.

With the utmost caution Thorne peered around the door. At once he saw the wooden kitchen chair in the middle of the room. His gaze travelled upwards: stockinged legs, a red skirt, white blouse—and Miranda's terrified face. Her hands were bound behind her back, and her mouth was gagged. A thin wire was looped around her neck and attached to a hook in the ceiling above. If the chair were kicked away her death would be horrific.

The details of what happened next would forever remain confused in Thorne's memory. Maybe the floor creaked as he shifted his weight. Maybe Miranda made an inarticulate sound through her gag. Maybe some sixth sense warned John Taylor. At any rate, as Thorne, crouching low, came into the room, Taylor turned and fired. To those outside, the answering report from Thorne's gun sounded like an echo.

Both men were hit. Taylor fell, blood quickly staining the front of his shirt. The shotgun pellets knocked Thorne back against the wall and he lost his revolver, which skittered across the room. As he made to retrieve it, he saw Taylor edging himself along the carpet and knew that he would never reach the gun in time. One of Taylor's long legs was already flexing to kick away the chair.

With an outraged cry Thorne flung himself on Taylor, forcing him away from the chair by the weight of his attack. But Taylor was a bigger, heavier man than Thorne and, in spite of his desperation, Thorne soon realized that he had lost the initiative and that once again Taylor was almost within reach of the chair. With a supreme effort, blood pouring from the pellet wounds, Thorne pulled himself upright and clutched Miranda's body, supporting it as Taylor kicked the chair away and fell back, dead.

This was how the police found them when, seconds later, they burst into the room.

CHAPTER 20

It was a week before Detective-Superintendent George Thorne was allowed to go home, a week that he thoroughly enjoyed. If he had to be in hospital, he couldn't imagine a better arrangement. Dr. Band had insisted that Miranda, after her ordeal, should also be hospitalized, and they shared a room, a room full of flowers and fruit and get-well cards.

Thorne had been lucky. He had not been severely wounded, and none of the shotgun pellets had penetrated any vital organs. Nevertheless, there had been a fair num-

ber to be extracted, and the Superintendent was glad of
the rest. He felt stiff and sore and very tired but, with
Miranda safe and well in the bed beside him, incredibly
happy.

It had been decided in the circumstances not to prose-
cute Myra Taylor, who claimed that she had been acting
under duress, and was in any case on the verge of a nervous breakdown. This suited Midvale and the Thames
Valley Force very well, because it meant that the affair
received surprisingly little publicity. True, a police officer
had shot a civilian, but it was obvious that the routine
inquiry would clear Superintendent Thorne of any blame.

At the Headquarters of the Thames Valley Police,
Thorne had become something of a hero, and his wife was
quite definitely a heroine. The Superintendent's determination, his continued belief in Miranda, were all discussed
at length; no officer in the Force would ever snigger about
Thorne's uxorious devotion again. As for Miranda, her
calm under stress and her brilliant effort to provide a clue
to her whereabouts soon became known, as did Thorne's
flash of inspiration concerning the crossword and Ot-
Moor.

It was not often that the Chief Constable admitted pub-
licly—or at least within the Force—that he had been
wrong and one of his supers right. Visiting the Thornes, he
had been magnanimous. He had apologized to them both,
and assured Miranda that she owed her life solely to
Thorne's determination and bravery. Then, with the Superintendent's permission, he had torn up his resignation.

Once these formalities were over, the Chief Constable
had said, "One can only suppose that Taylor's motive was
to make you suffer because he held you responsible for his
son's death. But he seems to have chosen a pretty compli-
cated way of setting about it."

Thorne replied, "I've been thinking about that, too, sir.
I could understand it if he'd just tried to kill me, but I
agree it's hard to believe that any sane man would go to

such devious lengths. I guess the answer is that Taylor wasn't altogether sane. Oh, he was probably sane enough in the legal sense, perhaps. But we know he doted on his son, and I guess the boy's crime and his death and the subsequent publicity—especially the fuss over the petition—deranged him. Of course we don't know what he had in mind eventually, but for my book I believe he intended to make me suffer hell before killing Miranda and himself. I think he always knew it would come to that in the end, but he didn't care as long as he got his revenge."

"Revenge." The Chief Constable shook his head. "Do you think that the Mulls—and Burwash and Parker—were similarly motivated?"

"If the word isn't too pretentious for what Eddie Mull calls kids' stuff on the part of Burwash and Parker—the glasshouse and orchid nonsense, the damage to Lady Farling's car, yes, sir," Thorne said. "But as for the Mulls I guess any thought of revenge was incidental. They needed money for their mother, you know, and if they could get it and pay off a grudge at the same time, all to the good."

"It's lucky the Mulls can't come up before Sir Leo," Miranda put in. "He'll never forgive them for poisoning Jason, quite apart from his houseman's death."

"Yes, indeed," said Midvale. "And incidentally, I was asked by Sir Leo and Lady Farling to give you their best wishes. Sir Leo has withdrawn the complaint he made, and I'm sure you'll be glad to know that Stephen Crispin has come clean. You were right, George. He's finally admitted he could identify Gloria Mull—and he's agreed to be a prosecution witness. He says if he'd done what you suggested in the beginning he'd never have been attacked and injured. And with his evidence added to the rest, the case against the Mulls is open and shut, thank God."

Miranda opened her mouth to make another comment, but Thorne forestalled her.

"So it's *All's Well That Ends Well,*" he said, beaming at his wife as he managed to produce a literary reference.

ABOUT THE AUTHOR

John Penn is a pseudonym which conceals a dual identity. John Penn himself was born in England and educated in London and at Oxford University. After many years of traveling widely as a government official, he turned his attention to collaborating with his wife on a series of crime novels set in London and the English countryside, which has been translated into many languages and has received considerable acclaim. American comments on previous John Penn books include "a stunning new suspense novel," "one of the best mysteries in months," "its suspense is excellent, its people engaging," "part menace, part mystery—delivered in Penn's effectively plain, straightforward style."

John Penn's wife is Palma Harcourt, the well-known author of novels of international espionage and intrigue. Together, they now make their home in Jersey in the Channel Islands.